Paved With Good Intentions

Book Two: The Nick Decker Series

DICK DENNY

Foundations Book Publishing Company
Brandon, MS 39047
www.foundationsbooks.net

Paved With Good Intentions
Book Two: The Nick Decker Series
By: Dick Denny

Cover by: Dawné Dominique
Edited by: Steve Soderquist
Copyright 2018© Dick Denny

Published in the United States of America
Worldwide Electronic & Digital Rights
Worldwide English Language Print Rights

ISBN: **978-1-64583-002-3**

Acknowledgements

Got to give credit to Mike Piscopo, Timothy Keeth, Kevin Harrison, and Daniel "Doc Doom" Button... my Medics.

Dedication

To Pete Abrams, for being the best writer in the world.

To John Ringo, for telling me "Grunt stories need to be told."

And to every Grunt out there. Especially the men of 3rd Platoon, Bravo Company, 1/505 PIR. For, as in the immortal words of Sgt Alvin J. Fields. "M#$H3R F~<KER, IF YOU AIN'T F~<KING AIRBORNE YOU AIN'T M#$H3R F~<KING SH!T"

Table of Contents

"Stay smart. Stay cool. It's time to prove to your friends that you're worth a damn. Sometimes that means dying. Sometimes it means killing a whole lot of people."

Dwight McCarthy, Frank Miller's Sin City Vol: 3 "The Big Fat Kill"

Prologue : Disappointed Mothers

Her voice held the icy tone that could only be carried by a cryogenic containment unit filled with liquid nitrogen, or a disappointed mother.

"Do you have any last words, Nick?"

Why would anyone ask that?

The hardwood floor was oddly rough under my palms. My knuckles were strangely sore, not that I'd have to worry about them cracking and scabbing over. I spat a hock of blood onto the hardwood before me, the red making a black smear against the cool teak. I felt the steel edge of the executioner's blade against the back of my neck, just above the collar of my dress shirt but below my hair line. Instead of thinking, *I'm about to get my fucking head chopped off*, my thought was: *That is uncomfortably fucking cold.*

"You really think I'm not going to fuckin' wreck your world?" I tried to growl, but it's hard to growl when you got a mouthful of blood.

I felt the angle of the blade on the back of my neck slightly shift.

"Do you really think you're in a position to make threats?"

"Promises, bitch."

I felt a string of blood drip from the corner of my mouth. "Fucking promises..."

"You brought this onto yourself." Again, she hit me with the disapproving, disappointed mommy tone. Joke was on her; with my life, I had grown immune to the disappointed mom voice. I couldn't help but chuckle.

"Social Distortion song."

"Excuse me?" she asked, almost pleasantly.

I tried to smile as the name of the song came to me.

"*Story of My Life.*"

Apparently she wasn't going to monologue, and she was tired of my pithy conversation.

"Last words, Decker."

Last words are a fucked up thing. Most people don't realize they're about to have their last words. I guess we always assume there is more time for that kind of thing. I knew I was on the spot.

"*If You Know What I Mean,* by Neil Diamond," I belatedly add: "Worthless, goddamned bitch."

She shook her head and her fingers milked the grip of the blunt tipped executioner's sword in her hands.

"Really? Neil Diamond?" She obviously ignored the profanity aimed at her. Fuck Shakespeare for setting the bar on last lines so fucking high. For every *The Rest is Silence* there are a thousand *What Bus's?* I guessed I could have, and should have gone with, *The Rest is Silence*.

Goddamnit.

They had no way of knowing this was not even near the worst thing that had happened to me that day.

Chapter One: May You Live in Interesting Times

Banditos by The Refreshments

T he great Chinese curse, as it's been explained to me, is *May you live in interesting times.* The problem is, what the crap does "interesting" mean? Some people find Jane Austen interesting...I don't. I find the German East Africa Campaign of World War One as fought by Lieutenant Colonel turned General Paul Emil von Lettow-Vorbeck fascinating, and I realize that statement would put some people to sleep, so what the hell is "Interesting?" Is the eternal argument of crochet versus knitting interesting? Is a survey of the placement Victorian end tables interesting? Is a movie starring legendary Hollywood badass Steve McQueen interesting? Yes. The last one is definitely a yes. So, besides watching *Bullet, The Getaway, The Magnificent Seven, The Great Escape*, etc...what was an example of, "Interesting Times?"

I don't know why my natural reaction was to pull the 1911 from under my suit jacket and shoot through the glass front door of the convenient store, past the clerk, and shatter the out-of-date security camera. But that's exactly what I did. The tempered glass of the front door turned into a spider web of lines through the formerly clear material all growing from a nearly half-inch hole created by the bullet. Jammer pulled the door back and I went in with the pistol leveled at the clerk.

The name on his shirt read *Sonny*, but I was willing to bet that wasn't the name the Arab-looking dude behind the counter was born with.

"Hands up." I said this gently, as trying to project calm seemed like a good idea—at the time, anyway. "Don't do anything stupid."

He nodded and had his hands up, fingers by his ears. He was visibly shaking. I would've felt bad for the guy were we not in too big of a hurry for that kind of thing. He stepped toward the register and started reaching for it.

"The fuck are you doing?" I asked, confused as the sights on my pistol followed him.

"The register."

He might have had an Arab look, but his voice was totally Southern California. Even with his voice quivering like a dying leaf as a storm rolls in, he sounded like the type of guy who would spring an erection when he heard The Red Hot Chili Peppers.

Gretchen followed me in with an apologetic look on her face. She was wearing a tight, gray tank top that didn't quite meet her cut-off short shorts or pouch belt. She had on her leather half jacket and polished jungle boots. In her left hand, she carried two large, brown paper grocery bags in their flattened form.

She looked to the clerk. "I am so sorry about this."

Jammer came last, letting the door close behind him and clicking the lock before turning the open sign around, even with the now opaque window a person wouldn't have been able to see it. He smiled jovially as only Jammer could. "Do you have Taqitos?"

Sonny now looked more confused than ever. That look made him look even more scared as he stared cross-eyed down the barrel of my pistol. The look on his face made me want to laugh, but that would have been a dick move.

"Jammer," Gretchen said politely. "We're on a mission, aren't we?"

It has always amazed me how much such a nerdy, ninja-trained stripper could totally mom-tone Jammer and get him back on track. I always had to resort to snapping and yelling.

So, here is the sad fact about the service industry, or at least as I saw it: It was quicker to rob the place for what we needed than it was to go in and ask politely for the clerk to go in the back and get what we'd needed.

Gretchen moved up and down some rows then asked. "Where are the cinnamon buns?"

"What?" Sonny mumbled, confused.

Jammer looked at his phone. "Not cinnamon buns, honey buns. We need Honey Buns; according to the internet, anyway." He put his phone up and started roving the aisles before stopping by a cooler and pulling out a bottle of Gatorade, then put it back and continued walking along the aisle nonchalantly for a man who, as Gretchen put it, was on a mission.

"Sonny," I said calmly down the sights of my pistol. "Look at me. Okay, I know the gun is scary, but it's cool. We just want the Honey Buns and we're getting out of here, all right?"

I heard the first of the flat paper bags open and Gretchen call out proudly, "Found them!"

"Me too!" Jammer added from the other end of the shop. He had found his Taqitos. So, we were robbing the shop for more than Honey Buns. Why not?

"I have ten," Gretchen said with concern in her voice. "Do we need more than ten?"

"How the fuck should I know?" I asked as calmly as anyone could while committing a felony. Which for me, is apparently pretty calmly.

"Sonny?" Gretchen asked as she walked up and put the bag of Honey Buns down by my feet. "Do you have more in the back?"

"What?" Sonny looked at her as if she'd just asked him advanced graduate level math.

She pulled one of the Honey Buns out of the bag and showed him. "Are there more of these in the back?"

He nodded and pointed to the door to the back by the coolers. "Second—no, third shelf."

She put the Honey Bun back in the bag then leaned up to kiss me on the cheek, then smiled sweetly to Sonny. "Thanks, Sonny, we'll be out of your hair in a minute."

She ran through the door into the back with the empty paper bag.

I tried to alleviate some of Sonny's confusion. "She likes paper bags because they're recyclable but aren't as pretentious as canvas tote style bags."

"What?" Sonny answered, or asked, depending on how you wanted to take it, as if I'd asked him to explain the fallacy of Malthusian equations in a post-industrial world.

"Never mind, buddy." I smiled, the barrel of my gun aimed right between his eyes. "We'll be out of here in a second."

He again reached for the register.

"What are you doing Sonny?" I asked.

"The cash drawer—"

"Buddy, we've covered this. We're not here for the cash." I smiled. Sonny was the textbook definition of an unreliable witness. He'd remember us wearing masks, then not, then yes... We'd all be over six feet, even though I was the tallest at five-foot-eight. "We just want Honey Buns."

"Honey Buns?" he stammered.

"And Taqitos!" Called out Jammer around a mouthful of his booty. "And a club soda!"

The aim of the pistol dropped from between Sonny's eyes to his mouth as I sighed. "Come on, Jammer..."

"What?" he asked as he came up with two Taqitos wrapped up in a piece of red-and-white-checkered paper and an open can of club soda.

"How do you drink that?" I asked, disgusted.

He shrugged. "If I spill something on my shirt, I'm prepared."

I couldn't tell if that was idiotic or genius so, like a fart in a crowded elevator, I let it go.

Gretchen came out of the back. "I got fifteen more. Twenty-five going to be enough?"

"Again," I sighed, "how am I supposed to know?"

"Internet doesn't say," Jammer offered.

"It'll have to do," I said, and miraculously, that was accepted by all parties.

I saw Gretchen's eyes dart over Jammer's head as he stood in his dark brown pants and Nerf-Herder T-shirt. She calmly sat the bag down and ambled down the aisle and opened a cooler. "Want a Dr Pepper?"

I knew we should be going, but if we were thieving...well, in for a penny, and all that. "Yeah, why not. Get me a Cherry Dr Pepper."

"Cherry?" She sounded confused. "Why?"

"I'm trying to be more health conscious. I need more fruit in my diet." Sonny didn't look any less confused as I gave my explanation.

Jammer sat up on the counter and leaned back looking at the rack above it. "I've been telling him he should be taking better care of himself for years." He smiled and nudged Sonny with his elbow before reaching up and grabbing two cans of Grizzly Long Cut.

"That actually makes a lot of sense," Sonny agreed, and I immediately began rethinking all the life choices I'd made in the last two minutes. Often, I've found people agreeing with me as a sure sign I'm jacked up.

Jammer hoped down and ambled away. I could hear him grabbing another Taqitos and wrapping it in the red-and-white checked paper, then pulling another club soda from the cooler.

Gretchen sat the bottles of Dr Pepper products on the counter. "Where are the security tapes?"

"It's a hard drive," Sonny corrected her.

"Okay, can you hand me those four cans of lighter fluid and a lighter, please." Her voice and demeanor were as sweet as the Honey Buns we were stealing.

He grabbed the things she asked for with his left hand, his right hand still quivering by his ear. I was getting tired of holding the pistol on him, but I knew if I lowered it he might focus on things other than the hole in the barrel. I didn't want him focusing on things like our faces or whatnot. I was not going to do ten to fifteen for Taqitos, club soda, lighter fluid, a lighter, two Dr Peppers, and twenty-five Honey Buns.

Gretchen asked, "Sweetie, Sonny, where is the hard drive for the security camera?"

"The office by—"

She moved with a purpose to the back. Jammer came back and leaned against the counter and munched on another Taqito as sounds of destruction started to echo from the back office. I would have guessed crowbar but knowing she didn't have one, I figured Gretchen was making short work to the security camera's computer and hard drive with her jungle boots. She didn't make any cute karate or kung fu sounds, which was a bit of a letdown. The sounds that did come from the office were that of Mongols and Vikings and the lovely testaments they left in their wake. I was certain the Huns would have made Gretchen their queen, if not their goddess of destruction.

Jammer smiled to the visibly shaken Sonny. "That's his girlfriend." He gestured at me with his half-eaten snack. "Hot, huh?"

Sonny literally stuttered out every word. "N—not really m—m—my type."

Jammer looked confused. "You into dudes?"

Sonny nodded.

Jammer jumped up and moved next to me. "Good, so tell us, objectively, please. Which of us is more handsome, and which one of us is roguish, and which is rugged. Go."

I didn't blame Sonny the confusion on his face. It was well earned and natural.

"Go on," Jammer pressed.

"I—I—I... dunno," Sonny stammered.

"Jammer, he can't be objective right now."

"Why not?" Jammer sounded disappointed and crammed the rest of his treat in his mouth.

"Cause I have a goddamned gun in his fucking face, man. Come on." I sounded a little exasperated because I didn't think I should have had to explained that.

Jammer tapped the pistol slide with his can of club soda. "Would this affect your decision?"

Sonny nodded fervently.

Jammer sighed. "That's a shame."

Gretchen came out of the back cheerily. "Well, gang, we should go." She batted her lashes at Sonny. "Your office has a fire in the garbage can, by the way." She picked up our Dr Peppers and one of the bags of Honey Buns in the other and glided effervescently out the door with a polite. "Thanks, Sonny. Have a nice day."

Jammer picked up the other bag and followed her. "We should rob a liquor store next!" He then laughed and exited.

I started moving sideways to the door, pistol still trained on the galvanization of confused and terrified clerk's face.

"So," he stammered, "you're not robbing the place?"

"We did," I admitted. "But we just needed the Honey Buns and we're in a hurry. In retrospect, it would have just been quicker to pay for them, I guess." I pushed the door open with my back and rolled out.

Behind me, as the broken door was shutting, I heard Sonny grumble. "Fuck this job, if you're not taking the money, I will."

We'd committed armed robbery for Honey Buns because armed robbery was quicker. I wondered what exactly were interesting times? I figured Jammer, Gretchen, and I were probably fucked.

Chapter Two: I'm Not a Veterinarian!

The Perfect Drug by Nine Inch Nails

We drove about half a mile from the convenient store and pulled into a strip mall and whipped around the back. The three of us piled out of Jammer's pickup truck and he quickly ran to the rear, throwing open the truck box then started rooting around while Gretchen and I dumped the twenty-five Honey Buns on the tailgate and started ripping the packaging open.

"What do ya think, Jammer?" I asked in a state of frantic calm, opening a Honey Bun and setting it on one of the half-flattened paper bags as Gretchen did the same next to me. She was humming a tune I couldn't place. That got annoying fast.

Jammer pulled up a bulging gallon-sized Ziploc bag and set it aside, then grabbed another equally burst-worthy bag. Both bags contained pills. "I got a bunch of Percocet and a bunch of Ambien."

He sat those bags on the wheel-well, then looked back into the truck box. "Oh, and I found an old joint."

He smiled as he pulled the rumpled baggy from the truck box. He dropped the baggy with the nonchalance of one who could make littering cool and pushed the end of the old joint between his bearded lips.

Gretchen ran and grabbed the bags of Percs and Ambiens and ran them to the tail gate, opening them. She grabbed a handful of each and dumped them by the Honey Buns we were stacking. She was still humming, and I kept wondering what the hell the song was. I knew I knew it.

Jammer patted his pockets trying to find a cigarette lighter.

Gretchen took one of the opened Honey Buns and started pushing a random mix of pills into it, marring the pristine glazed surface.

"Jammer," she said, not looking up.

"Yeah?" he said around the joint as he reached back into the cab of the truck and found a disposable Bic lighter in one of the door slots.

"How many should we use?" She paused in her literal pill-pushing.

He lit the lighter and sparked up the end of the joint. He inhaled and coughed. "God, that's some skanky fucking weed." He held it between his fingers and looked up to Gretchen as he shrugged. "I dunno."

Gretchen's jaw metaphorically hit the floor. "What the hell, Jammer...this was your idea!"

He took another hit of the joint, and again coughed. "Yeah, I came up with the idea. I didn't engineer the fucking thing."

She looked down to the drug-filled Honey Bun. "What if we use too much and kill it?"

I kept ripping open Honey Buns and methodically stacking them. One problem at a time, and I could handle this one.

Again, Jammer coughed.

"I'm not a veterinarian."

He took another hit and coughed. He didn't offer Gretchen or I any because he knew we didn't roll that way. Gretchen and I might drink like fishes at times, but that was the extent of our substance abuse.

I stopped opening Honey Buns long enough to pull my flask out of my pocket and unscrew the lid. I took a long slow tug off it and enjoyed the smooth warm elixir that was the Macallan 18. I smiled as I started screwing the lid back and smirked at to Gretchen. "You've been humming, *Take It On The Run,* by REO Speedwagon?"

She tore he annoyed gaze from Jammer and smiled as she looked up to me. "Close. *Take It On The Run* is by Starship. But good catch, babe."

She leaned up and gave me a kiss.

I cocked my head to the side. "No, it's definitely REO Speedwagon." I started tearing open Honey Buns again.

"Yeah," Jammer tossed in with a hacking cough. "It's REO Speedwagon."

I shot a glance to Jammer. "Jammer, if the weed is so shit, stop smoking it."

He smiled and took another long pull off it. "Its skank weed, but waste not, want not. Am I right?"

"Jammer," I said slowly, the way I did when Jammer was distracted, and I needed to drag him back on task. "You are an 18 Delta man. You did veterinarian shit."

He took a long draw from the skank weed, hacked, spit, exhaled, and smiled. "I did, didn't I?" He smiled wistfully. "But this stuff doesn't apply." Jammer gestured at the glazed breakfast snacks offhandedly. "Just pack those fuckers and we'll deal with any problems later."

Gretchen's eyes met with mine and we both sighed in resignation. It was the best we were going to get, and we both knew it.

She started loading Honey Buns with ten to fifteen pills each. If we weren't being scientific about it, why would it matter? She started stuffing the pill-laden Honey Buns into one of the empty brown paper bags as I kept stacking opened Honey Buns on the other.

"You want to get over here and help, Jammer?" I asked without looking up from my work.

He leaned against the truck, enjoying his horrible quality weed. "I did help."

"How?" Gretchen asked, dropping another Honey Bun in the bag.

He leaned his head back. "My idea, my product."

He had a point, so we didn't belabor the point. Wanting to change the subject before Jammer decided to charge us for all the drugs we were using, I nudged Gretchen with my elbow as we both worked. "What do I get if it's REO Speedwagon."

She deposited another laced Honey Bun in the bag. "I'll forever fast forward through the intro-credits of The Big Bang Theory."

"Done," I quickly agreed.

"What do I get when you realize it's Starship?" she asked with a cocky smile.

"I'll concede that down is the proper position for a toilet seat." It was an easy offer, because I was certain I was right.

"Done." She grinned and cackled like a witch. "Jammer, you witness?"

Jammer stood straight and faced up, shoulders back and with the grave formality of a warden reading the execution order repeated from memory. "I, Jammer, have witnessed the wager between Gretchen and Nick. Both parties have approved the stakes of which. May God have mercy on your souls." He then went back to leaning against the side of the truck. "This is a bad idea," he said offhandedly.

"Jammer, this is your fucking plan." I opened the last of the Honey Buns and grabbed a random assortment of pills, joining Gretchen in the stuffing.

"What... am I not allowed to recognize flaws in a plan because it's my plan?" he asked, perturbed.

"You can. You have every right to," Gretchen diplomatically countered. "But it's not real confidence inspiring, is it?"

He thought about it for a few moments. He dropped the nub of the joint and crushed it out with his shoe as if it was a cigarette and he was James Dean. "Never mind. This plan is flawless." He smiled and walked back to the tailgate. "It's totally gonna work. Sure as the sun comes up, blah blah blah."

I sighed. "That was good up to the end, buddy."

Gretchen nodded in agreement. "I was brimming with confidence until the blahs."

Jammer picked up a Percocet and popped it in his mouth. He picked up a Honey Bun and took a bite. Then he took the rest of it and started pushing pills into it with the perfection of a stippling artist with OCD.

Jammer pushed pills into four Honey Buns before he stopped and went back to the truck box. He dug around until coming up with a smile. He held a bottle of hand sanitizer in his left hand and a plastic container of baby wipes in the other. He sat the hand sanitizer on the truck box and calmly pumped four or five pumps into his cupped hand. The sticky slick sound assaulted our ears as he began spreading it around on his hands. He had used more hand sanitizer than a not particularly bright child would. My hands were sticky from handling so many Honey Buns but it seemed less disgusting than Jammer smearing the hand sanitizer, so copious that it fell in large globs on the concrete before him.

"Thanks for the help, Jammer," I said as I kept stuffing pills in the pastry.

"It's what I do," he said cheerfully as he began wiping his hands and forearms with a handful of baby wipes. He dropped the baby wipes on top of the crushed joint corpse.

"Is this going to work?" Gretchen whispered, dropping another laden Honey Bun in the bag.

I shrugged. "It's more of a plan than we normally have. So who knows?" To be fair, or normal plan for us was some variation of 'wing it,' so this actually felt as structured as Operation Overlord.

"Maybe we should start working on that," she offered with a quizzical look.

I chuckled. "You want to mess with success, babe?"

She laughed. "Babe."

We'd started calling each other that as a way to make fun of a couple at a restaurant we saw doing that.

Babe.

Yeah, babe?

I love you, babe.

I love you too, babe.

Should we get some appetizers, babe?

Babe, only if you want, babe.

Babe, I could kill some Bruschetta.

Babe, then we're getting some Bruschetta, babe.

I love you, babe.

It was so easy to mock. Easy to mock but not so easy that we felt bad mocking people like that. Because frankly, we certainly didn't feel bad making fun of those types at all. The problem is in the course of mocking those couples we became inoculated to it. So thank God we weren't dropping 'babe' into every address to the other, but they were slipping in there with a sickeningly familiar regularity. We both accepted it probably wasn't going to go away.

"You two are cute." Jammer chuckled as he watched us. "Gretchen, you're my favorite of any of Nick's girlfriends."

"Ahhh, thanks Jammer." Her smile was sweet. Then again, it always sweet for Jammer. They'd really bonded when he'd rescued her from the Teutonic Knights, or maybe it was when he talked her through pulling a bullet out of my shoulder. She then turned her juxtaposed dark eyed yet bright gaze on me. "Who was your favorite girlfriend before me?"

I felt like a fox standing at the door to the hen house with a bib. "Alison."

She ribbed me with her elbow. "Who's Alison?"

I sighed. "There *was* Alison, and here's the thing. I thought the girl was seventeen. Instead, she was eighteen but looked sixteen and told me she was twenty-three."

She looked at me for a second then turned her head up to the sky. "Hey!" she yelled, and this time elbowed me in the rips drawing a *umph* from me. "That's from a Stroke-9 song, you asshole!"

I laughed. She always caught me. I didn't mind.

I dropped the last drug-laden Honey Bun in the bag. Jammer held out the bottle of hand sanitizer putting one squirt in her hand then mine. Apparently, he didn't think we needed as much as he did. We rubbed it around then took a baby wipe from him. Jammer put up the hand sanitizer and the remainder of the gallon Ziplocs of pills while we wiped our hands with the baby wipes.

Gretchen looked around and then ran to a dumpster to throw her wipe away. She ran back got mine and used it to pick up Jammer's pile before dumping it in the plastic bag she stuffed the Honey Bun wrappers in, depositing it all in the dumpster.

Jammer jumped behind the wheel of the truck and I held the door so she could climb in the middle. I handed her the bag of drugged sweets, then hopped in the passenger seat.

Jammer had his phone in his hand typing with his thumb as he started the truck. He held the phone over for Gretchen and I to see. "*Take It On The Run*, REO Speedwagon," he said nonchalantly as he put the phone up and got the truck going.

"Son of a bitch..." Gretchen groaned as we got moving.

Chapter Three: Like Aloe On A Sunburn

Over My Head by Lit

I t was a half empty lot, half preliminary construction site, and one hundred percent creepy as shit. There were piles of construction materials strewn about a field with places of bare dirt and others knee-high grass. Jammer turned off the lights, gunned the engine, and rammed the chain-link gate going about thirty-five miles per hour. The lock holding it burst and the gate flew open as we skidded to a stop, dust billowing before us in a cloud.

"Are we sure it's here?" Gretchen asked as I held the door for her. She handed me the bag with our pill-laden Honey Buns. I took the bag and put it on the hood as Jammer jumped out and started putting a harness on his head. It gripped like a band and had a strap going over the top.

Out in the field, a twenty-pound bag of cement mix arched through the air and exploded as it hit a pallet of bricks. Oddly, that was less distracting than what Jammer was doing.

"Jammer?" I asked cautiously, not sure if I wanted an answer or not.

"Yeah buddy?" he replied cheerfully as he adjusted the head harness.

"Whatcha doing?"

"I'm putting on a Go-Pro, man." He answered as if it were the most obvious thing in the world. His reply was coated in a tone that implied I was an idiot for having asked. "I'm recording some of this hero shit for posterity. I mean, this could be a big hit on YouTube."

I started at him blankly. Gretchen shook her head as Jammer affixed his camera to the mounting harness on his head. "What?" he scoffed. "There's money in that shit, or depending on how things go, we could put it on America's Funniest Videos."

"So," I spoke slowly. Out in the field, another twenty-pound bag of concrete arched at least thirty feet through the air before bursting as it landed on its corner. "We have a plan that we're not sure is going to work, and you want to record it, because it might be funny?"

"It's dark. What are you going to do about that?" Gretchen asked. Apparently, she didn't have a problem of getting the footage and using it for fun and profit. Her issue was solely technical.

Jammer bit his lip as a stack of plywood slid like a deck of cards spilling across a table. He took off the mount and tossed it on the seat of the truck, muttering obscenities. I managed to make out "Cocksucking, goddamn, mother fucking shit..." the rest was lost in a sea of profane adjectives.

"What about the music?" Jammer asked as he came back around. Gretchen was making three stacks of pill-bearing Honey Buns on the hood.

I pulled out my phone and tossed it to him. "Take your pick."

Jammer started scrolling through my phone's selection of music. "Jesus Christ, Nick," he muttered sadly.

"What?"

"Well first off, you should really put a passcode on your phone." Had the judgment in his voice been a blanket, it would have kept a body warm all winter.

"Who would want to steal the shit on my phone?" I asked as I watched a stack of PVP pipe scatter like twigs.

Jammer's jaw dropped in disbelief. "For crying out loud, think about whose damned phone numbers are in here, Nick. Seriously?"

I wasn't about to admit that he had a valid point. After his Go-Pro silliness, I wasn't conceding that he might be right about anything.

"And secondly," he grumbled. "You know there are other bands besides AC/DC."

"Yeah," I admitted. "AC/DC and other bands that fucking wished they *were* AC/DC."

Gretchen grinned. "Amen."

Jammer shook his head as if he were the exasperated one. "We need soothing music, Nick... soothing. You know what soothing is, right?"

"Like aloe on a sunburn?" I offered.

He nodded slowly in the affirmative. "Like aloe on a sunburn. That's right, Nick. Good..."

Once again, I felt Jammer was treating me like a puppy. I didn't know whether I should be touched by the level of affection, or offended because I wasn't a goddamned dog.

"Fuck it," he muttered. "I'm gonna buy some music on your phone. What's your password?"

I sighed. It didn't seem a fight worth having. "H, minus, capital H, capital M."

Jammer chuckled even as he shook his head in disapproval while looking for soothing music to purchase.

"Okay." Gretchen smiled. She had completed two stacks of eight Honey Buns and one stack of nine. "We only got two bags, though."

I took one of the two paper bags and dumped the stack of nine into it. I wanted dibs before I ended up with a sticky shirtsleeve trying to balance them without the bag.

Jammer didn't look up from my phone. "Just leave my stack on the hood."

Gretchen nodded and put her pile of eight into the second brown grocery bag.

"If that's the case, Jammer, you anchor here. Gretchen and I will work the field." I looked to both their faces to make sure they both understood the plan. They both looked up briefly to express the level of comprehension a plan this stupid deserved.

Gretchen leaned up and gave me a quick kiss. Somehow, she could calm me down and rile me up all at the same moment. don't think I've ever minded saying I was a definitely a fan of this interesting phenomenon.

"Strength and honor, bro," Jammer grumbled as he still searched through music. Then he needlessly added, "What are you waiting for? I'm not kissing ya."

Gretchen and I took our bags and headed out into the field. I started walking toward the middle while Gretchen swung wide around the fence line.

"Got it!" Jammer exclaimed before getting in the truck to pair my phone with it. He turned up his speakers that were definitely not factory standard. I heard the opening notes tinkle from piano ivories.

"What is this?" I called back. It was familiar, and then it hit me. I smiled. "Never mind. Good choice."

"Thanks, man. Great song, right?" Jammer asked, laughing.

"Hell to the fucking yeah," I agreed.

"What song is it?" Gretchen asked as she cut wide around the field.

"Dan Hill's *Sometimes When We Touch*," Jammer yelled to her before taking a bite of one of his pill-laden Honey Buns.

"Jammer, you got to quit eating those, man," I yelled back to him. There were at least fifty meters between us, but that didn't stop me from being concerned for him. Even a professional chemical supplement experimenter like Jammer could slip up.

He chuckled. "Yeah, I forgot." That didn't stop him from swallowing anyway.

When the song got to the first chorus, that's when I noticed the first ripples in the air. For a moment, it looked like the special effects from the movie *Predator*. The rippled air seemed to shift and undulate. It was a bit disconcerting, but quickly solidified. Patches of solidity and color formed. It was a mess of black and reddish-brown fur, thick and tangled. It came more into view and it was clear it was at least twelve feet high, from first snout to tail stretching at least twenty-five to thirty feet. It had three heads, the far left—as I was facing it anyway—looked lab, the middle looked wolf, and the right looked pitbull. All six eyes burned a bright green like I imagined a baleful hellfire to look. Each head growled at a different pitch, making a cacophonous bedlam out of something that should have sounded vaguely normal.

So, there was a needed correction for the Cerberus Wikipedia article. Apparently, soothing music makes Cerberus visible, but doesn't really put it to sleep. Thanks, Orpheus, you piece of shit.

I reached my hand out with my palm facing it, trying to be non-threatening, wondering how the hell could I threaten that thing anyway?

"Good boy…"

Jammer yelled from the truck. "I can see its wang, Nick! So you're right, it's a boy… and *what a boy!*"

"Not helping, Jammer…" I was trying to keep eye contact with three sets of eyes at once.

I felt the tug in the back of my mind. I dropped the bag as I dove to the right and rolled as the wolf head snapped where I was a moment before. I rolled further as the pitbull head buried its snout in the grass where I had just passed.

I rolled back and managed to get to my feet in a crouch. I saw the paw coming and knew the odds were I wasn't dodging it. I planted my feet and caught it. The paw was larger than my chest, but I wrapped my arms tight around it, getting a good hold and felt it push me, digging my feet in deep and making furrows in the ground under me.

It would have killed a normal man, or a miscreant like Jammer.

"Nick!" Gretchen screamed.

"I'm okay," I grunted through gritted teeth.

I twisted and bent the paw an unnatural direction. I didn't break it, but Cerberus wasn't happy either. It moved and I saw the lab head coming straight for me.

I dropped the paw and stepped into it as I jabbed with my right. Its nose was warm, wet, and soft; my fist connected solidly to it. I'm not sure the punch hurt it at all, but at a minimum, the blow stunned and confused it. The other two heads moved in sympathetic concert as the lab head shook rapidly, and the whole body stumbled back.

I watched it warily and saw that it was regaining its footing. I sprinted to my dropped bag and pulled out a Honey Bun. The balefire eyes were drawn to the treat as if they'd been guided by radar.

I moved my hand with the Honey Bun in it left and right, watching the wicked eyes follow it. It seemed more interested in what I had than its holder—me—so that was good, right?

I tossed the Honey Bun toward the lab snout and it caught it mid-air. The jaws chomped far more enthusiastically than it needed to, given the comparative size of the Honey Bun to its mouth.

The lab head seemed happy but the other two growled and glowered. I pulled another Honey Bun out and tossed it. The wolf and pitbull heads snapped at each other before the wolf caught it with sadistic glee. I quickly threw a third before the pitbull decided I looked like a treat.

I heard the soft sound of dry grass being stepped on and glanced to my right. Gretchen was stepping closer to the definitely-not-normal dog. She held out a Honey Bun from her bag. The pitbull head took it from her hand without managing to take a finger with it. She smiled and petted the nose, and the head gobbled its treat.

Jammer came running over, grinning like a twelve-year-old who just discovered masturbation. He had his Honey Buns half crushed in his hands and held them up as a wad to the lab head. The dog started licking them from Jammer's hands.

The wolf head glowered and I moved close, and feeding him Honey Buns one at a time. The wolf's burning green eyes never lost the look of *I'm fucking onto you, asshole*, but it ate the Honey Buns all the same. Slowly, the massive beast settled down onto his belly, crossing its front paws under his heads.

Its breath did not smell sweet, but was a hot, sticky wet that one would associate with a burning village in a place like Laos or Cambodia.

The lab head was the first to start snorting, the pitbull quickly following. The long tail wrapped up under its body. The wolf head's burning eyes never really closed, but narrowed to slits. I would have felt better if it snored.

Jammer leaned in between the lab and wolf head and tried to take a selfie. Gretchen pressed into my side and wrapped her arm around my waist. I pulled her to me and we walked back to the truck. There I grabbed my phone and pulled up my uncle in my contacts.

I held the phone to my ear and smirked to Gretchen. She couldn't keep the grin off her face as she heard my half of the conversation. "Hey… yeah… Well, we finally got your fucking dog."

Chapter Four: The Biggest Regret of My Life Until A Couple Of Weeks Ago

Nimrod by Green Day

Pretty much every TV show taking place in the contemporary world features a hangout. It's either a diner or coffee shop or some such locale. I would have murdered someone for a cool little diner where I could get waffles and limp bacon, or a good burger and crispy fries. I don't like coffee. But even if I did, the Starbucks is overrun with hipster assholes writing their screenplays, novels and their next zine. Even before I felt the unfiltered Wrath of God in my gut I wanted to punch anyone in the face that used the term "zine." The good donut place just felt too clean for a good hangout. An old guy named Tim who hates Jammer with a passion runs the best burger stand in town, so that was out. There was a good hotdog cart, but it's constantly moving, no place to sit, and not open at two in the morning.

We found ourselves sitting in a booth at a place whose blinking, humming neon sign simply read *Eats*, and a smaller one under it flickering *Open* in a manner that left the open or closed nature of the place in question. The booth top had an oddly sticky feel regardless of how many times the waitress wiped it down with a rag reeking of bleach. There was a polished steel napkin holder that held napkins of a size that it was never engineered to accommodate. The silverware the waitress laid out was mismatched, probably collected from several restaurants. The plastic cups were different makes and shades.

The waitress had a bored, dispassionate look. Her hair had once been in a tight bun, but it was frayed and strands of once red hair stuck out wildly. She wore a uniform that would have been more suited for a diner in the 1950s and was worn and threadbare enough in various places to have been that old. She wrote on a pad with plain white paper with the word *Ticket* across the top; no lines or columns, just *Ticket*. She wrote with a mini pencil taken from a mini golf course.

"I want a burger with cheese, bacon, pickles, lettuce, but no tomato." Jammer became adamant, "I don't want anything red on the burger, except ketchup, and also mayo and mustard. What kind of mustard do you have?"

She sounded bored. "The yellow kind."

"Okay, that will do. I want fries and onion rings, too."

The waitress listened to all that and wrote *burger* on the pad.

Gretchen smiled to the waitress and didn't seem disappointed or perturbed that she never looked up from the pad or stopped chewing her gum. "I'll take the Ruben."

She wrote *Ruben*, not bothering to ask what sides Gretchen might want.

The waitress sighed and gestured to me with the pencil stub. "Are you going to order?"

"Pancakes."

She didn't write anything down and walked off, handing the piece of paper through the slit back to the kitchen. The cook got to work and the waitress sat behind the counter and picked up a crossword puzzle.

"This," Jammer whispered, "is going to be horrible or amazing. I can already tell there's going to be no middle ground."

Gretchen picked up her plastic cup of Dr Pepper and held it out like doing a toast. "To a job well done, boys."

I clinked my cup to hers and Jammer clinked with his coffee mug and sipped the stale brew.

Jammer asked, "Hey Nick, what did we get for finding Lucifer's freaking dog?"

"Well, he fixed my office door." I let that sink in for a moment. "He's also making sure there's no cop trouble from the whole...you know."

"The whole murdering a bunch of weird Christian bikers thing?" Jammer asked off-handed, not caring if anyone heard.

I sighed and nodded. "Yeah, that thing."

The bell by the door rang as it opened. Gretchen gasped and tightened up against my side, grabbing my arm as she saw the customer come through the door.

"Son of a bitch," I muttered.

I guess it says a lot about our lives that when someone comes through the door and makes eye contact, we automatically assume the worst. He was about Jammer's height, which put him a good two or three inches shorter than me, but had us on age by ten to fifteen years. The gray in his beard gave it away more than anything else. His beard was full and had a good shape to it; not a hipster douche beard, but an *I work with an axe for a living* beard. He wore a plaid flannel shirt and dark, heavy-duty denim slacks, a gray-and-black gortex jacket, and heavy work boots, definitely steel toed, that completed the outfit. His dark eyes seemed young, but suspicious. Those eyes became even more suspicious when they fell on me, and the back of Jammer's head. His features were sub-continental, but whether Pakistani or Indian was a distinction that neither Jammer nor myself had ever bothered to find out, but we were sure his folks were Indian, even though he was from Wisconsin.

I smiled to Gretchen and she raised an eyebrow as I did. "It's cool," I whispered into her hair. She smiled sweetly. Apparently, that was all that was needed to allay her concerns. I squeezed my arm around her and gestured for him to join us.

He started his way over and gestured to get the waitress's attention, telling her, "Coffee and a cup of chili."

Jammer's head snapped at the sound of the voice and he clapped his hands together. "Switch!"

I half stood and held out my hand. Switch gestured for me to sit, but shook my hand, nonetheless.

He slid into the booth next to Jammer. "You two," he said with no veiled annoyance, "are some aggravating bastards."

Gretchen giggled at that.

That caught Switch's attention and he looked to Gretchen in mild surprise. He'd realized she was there but hadn't really noticed her till now. He held out his hand to her. "I have a name, but I'm not sure these two even know it so for simplicity sake. Call me Switch." The only accent to his voice was a mix of Rocky Mountain and a little Wisconsin that would slip in on occasion but was so subtle it was more garnish than entree.

"I'm Gretchen." She smiled a smile that seemed demure to the casual observer, but the professional would see the mischievous glint to it.

They shook and Switch asked, "So, how do you know these two losers?" He gestured between Jammer and me affectionately.

"She's Nick's girlfriend," Jammer told him with a smile, as he held the coffee mug in front of his face trying to hide it.

Gretchen stuck her tongue out at Jammer. I was just happy he didn't play the soulmate card.

Switch looked confused and turned to me. "Did your cock grow four or five inches or did you all of a sudden become charming?"

She leaned in closer to my side resting her head on my shoulder. "I hope not...to both."

Switch's eyes darted between Gretchen and me suspiciously.

Jammer chuckled and nudged Switch with his elbow. "I totally saw Gretchen over there penetrate Nick in a very sore spot." He laughed and Switch look evolved from confused to disgusted. It looked like something was coming up but nothing did; I think the look was a little bit of dramatic playacting but who knows?

"Jammer!" Gretchen gasped. "You're so bad."

"So it's not true?" Switch asked with an obvious hope of confirmed negativity.

Gretchen looked to me and thought for a second. "Well, I guess the technical details are factually accurate."

Switch hit us with the *going to vomit* look again and that just drew more laughter out of Jammer. Switch shook his head as the waitress brought us our food.

Jammer's burger came out plain. On the plate was a slice of cheese still in its plastic wrapper, a pickle (not a slice of pickle but a whole pickle), one slice of lettuce that had a shred of carrot stuck to it making me think it as pulled from a salad, a half of the expressly forbidden tomato, a piece of bacon that was both cold and hard in the least appetizing manner. There were a smattering of fries and onion rings on the plate. Jammer picked up one of each and inserted the fry into the ring in a lewd manner that was as subtle the reaction given an Arab guy yelling "Allah Akbar" in a convention of American Iraq and Afghanistan veterans.

Gretchen seemed a touch disturbed as her Ruben was sliced across the middle instead of diagonally. There was something unnatural about it. "No sides?" She asked cautiously.

"You didn't ask for any." The waitress muttered matter-of-factly despite the fact she'd never given Gretchen a chance to ask for any sides.

She put down the pancakes in front of me. The bacon was as limp as a teenager overdosing on Viagra, and the sausage was slightly green.

Whatever was in the cup put in front of Switch was covered in so much shredded cheese it was completely covered and concealed.

There was no offered mustard, ketchup, or mayo for Jammer. There wasn't any butter or syrup offered to me.

Switch looked to the food on the table and shook his head. "I don't know why we're friends."

"What do you mean?" Jammer asked as he crammed the fry and ring combo in his mouth.

Switch looked to Jammer like it was the dumbest question he ever heard. "So you bastards invite me to town because you have some"—he made exaggerated air quotes—"*crazy shit going down.* So I come but do you offer me a place to stay? Oh I can stay with Jammer and have the DEA kick the door open and I lose my licenses and that costs me the only job I've ever had that I enjoy." To be fair Jammer did distribute illegal drugs. He then poked his accusatory finger at me. "I can stay with Nick, but he lives on a pull-out couch in his office and I am not going to be the Frank Reynolds to his Charlie Kelly."

"Actually I've been splitting it with him," Gretchen said in a consolatory manner. "So no room there."

"Great, great, thank you." Switch held his hands up in surrender. "So I come to town but end up in a hotel because I can't crash with my *buddies*. Then I ask what's going on and Jammer tells me to come here for"—he gestured at the cheese covered monstrosity before him—"this." He looked between Jammer and I. "You two suck."

Gretchen looked confused. "What do you mean lose your license?"

Switch slumped back and looked at the pile of cheese in defeat. "I'm licensed to purchase, transport, store, use..." He paused, "Basically I get to legally do shit with explosives."

"That's cool!" Gretchen leaned in. "What do you do?"

He pushed the cheese-covered abomination away from him without ever touching the spoon sticking out of the top. "I blow up buildings."

"What?" Gretchen's eyes were filled with all the light that was absent in Switch's defeated features.

He shrugged. "I've blown up a couple of buildings in Reno and Vegas. Old casinos. Making way for new resort-type places I guess." He brightened up a bit. "I did get to stay in a room Frank Sinatra stayed in at one point. Then blew it up the next day."

"That, might be the coolest story you have, man," I was forced to admit. I mean who doesn't love Frank Sinatra? Besides Richard Nixon, but he was dead so he doesn't count.

"Bullshit," Jammer argued as he took a bite of the burger, it was disturbingly juicy. When he set it down, you could still see the grind of the ground beef in it. I noticed this, Gretchen noticed as well, but Switch wasn't unaware of it. Jammer didn't seem to notice either though. "You know the best story."

I thought for a moment. "Him and the girl fuckin' up the bed in the Irish B&B with wine and leaving without ever registering and paying?"

Switch dropped his head and Jammer shook his. "Nope, motherfucking Iron Man."

I chuckled and Gretchen looked confused. Jammer looked to Gretchen and shrugged. "Long story." Then did nothing to elaborate.

I looked at my green sausage. "Can we just go now?"

Gretchen turned her eyes to her unnaturally cut sandwich. "Yes."

I dropped some cash on the tabletop as we got up to leave. All I wanted was a diner, or something similar. A place to sit in the same booth, have the attentive playful waitress ask me "the usual?" I got to the door and looked back in at the mismatched place and the disinterested waitress. I looked through the service slit into the kitchen. The cook was chubby with a splotchy face. I was pretty sure he was bald under his paper hat. His apron looked stained but surprisingly well pressed. He reached up and waved to me with his chubby hand. The fat of his fingers had half grown over his wedding ring. He waved with excited unalloyed enthusiasm.

I stepped back in and pulled a twenty out of my pocket. I walked behind the counter ignoring the disinterested waitress and held it through the service slat. "Thanks, man, it was great." I lied; he beamed and took the bill out of my hand with unabashed pride.

I walked out without another word.

That guy might have been the world's shittiest cook, but he was doing his best. He wasn't half-assing it, he was putting it all out there on the field, even if his best was grossly inadequate. A guy doing the best he could enthusiastically; they make sports movies about kids like that. That guy deserved better than his best, but we're all forced to play the hand we're dealt.

I got to the door and looked back, he waved with unabashed joy, like we were the best of friends. I pushed the door open with my back and gave him a wave. We never went back to that diner, I never saw the cook again, and I never told the others how big of a sucker I could be at times.

Chapter Five: Direction of Travel from the Frying Pan

Double Trouble by Lynyrd Skynyrd

It was almost three-thirty in the morning when Gretchen and I got back to Suite 3B, second floor of 505 Gavin Drive. The new door was in place and instead of reading *Decker Investigations;* the newly painted window read *N & G Investigators and Services Ltd.* Gretchen blushed when she saw it.

I shrugged as I worked my key into the lock. "Well, I figure we might as well be partners, right?"

I don't know if she agreed or not, but she did kiss me. So if she were unhappy she could stay freaking stay that way for all I cared.

I got the door open and we stepped in. There was a third desk in the front office now, right next to mine.

She walked over and ran her hands over some of the scars on the desktop. "I found it in one of the offices upstairs that no one was using and had it brought down for you."

She leaned back against it and crossed her arms. "I love it. No nameplate?"

I smirked as I shut the door locking it. "I don't know your last name."

She laughed.

"Can't have a nameplate that just reads *Gretchen*, right?" I turned and faced her across the dark office.

"Do you want to know it?" She asked quizzically.

"No.".

"Oh?" She cooed.

"Is it Decker?" I asked as I walked over and slipped my arms around her waist lifting her up off the desk to stand with me.

"No," she confessed as she shook her head.

"Then what's it going to change?" I asked as I brushed a strand of dark hair back behind her ear.

I held her close there for a bit and she breathed into the shoulder of my suit jacket. She looked up and I could tell she was smiling playfully even in the dark. She wasn't whispering, just that normal quiet tone people use in the dark. "We can fuck on the new used desk if you want."

I sighed. "I'd love to... but I'm fuckin' exhausted."

She chuckled. "Me too..."

We went to the back and changed. I pulled on a pair of flannel boxers and she changed into a camisole and pair of boy shorts. We didn't even get the pull-out bed pulled out. We simply lay back on the couch under my old poncho liner and held each other. The sweet oblivion of sleep hit us like a Mack truck.

The only reason I knew what time it was when my eyes opened is because Agnes poked her head through the door and said. "Mr. Decker, you have half an hour until your eleven o'clock appointment.

Gretchen and I pulled ourselves off the couch and took a quick, no hanky panky, you scrub my back, I scrub yours shower. I pulled on a gray suit and Gretchen tugged on a pair of gray yoga pants, a tank top, her pouch belt, and her half jacket. I knew that pouch belt had shuriken, but I wondered what else might be in those pouches?

I felt the weight of my pistol rig under my arms as I opened the door and headed out into the office. I sat at my desk and felt under it. I confirmed I had another 1911 under there just in case. I pulled it from its holster and half pulled back the slide until I could see the brass of a round in the chamber. I eased the slide back forward and thumbed back the hammer before putting it back in its hiding place.

Gretchen watched all this and then looked under her desk. The disappointment was plain as day on her face that there was no gun hidden under hers.

The door opened exactly as the clock hit eleven. She had golden blonde hair and bright blue eyes in a thin face with a sharp chin. She had a petite figure and was barely taller than Gretchen yet someone her gams didn't seem to quit as one poked through the slit in her white and gold dress. She had to unpin the wide-brimmed white hat atop her head and her hair fell in tight-coiled curls as Agnes came around her desk to take the lady's hat and white half cape.

"Welcome to D & G Investigations and Services Limited." Agnes smiled as she took the hat and cape hanging them on the old wooden hat stand in the corner. "I'm Agnes, is there anything I can get you, ma'am?"

I know at times a bit of my Southern accent pops through my mostly accent-less diction, but her accent was cloying as she smiled sweetly. "No, thank you, but it's so sweet of you to offer. Bless your heart."

Bless your heart… that could mean *you are such a sweet thing* or *you can go fuck yourself*. I didn't know this lady well enough to know which was which yet.

Agnes turned and held out a presenting a hand. "This is Mr. Decker, our senior investigator."

I stood and held out my hand across the desk. "Please, call me Nick. This is Gretchen, my partner." I gave Gretchen a nod. "What can we do for you?"

She walked over and she shook my hand with a soft hand and a limp grip. "I'm Gabrielle." She said it politely, but with a tone that insinuated that I should recognize the name.

"Have a seat." I gestured to one of the two seats in front of our desks.

She sat and demurely crossed her ankles and placed her hands on her knees. She was prim and proper enough to give Emily Post an erection. She looked between me and Gretchen, with her soft smile matching her eyes. "It's nice to see two souls find each other." She giggled. "I almost want to ask you two for an autograph."

My eyes narrowed and I felt my hand sliding under the desk toward the stashed pistol. "Who are you?" I asked with a hard edge to my voice. If this was going to go Game On I didn't see a reason to fuck around with pleasantries.

She cocked her head a little confused. "I'm Gabrielle, the Herald of The Throne."

Gretchen leaned back in her chair and crossed her arms. "I thought that was Gabriel."

"Pishhh..." Gabrielle waved dismissively more with her fingers than her whole hand. "That was a misprint."

"A misprint?" I found myself asking.

"Yes," her tone implied I was being silly even asking. "The Bible might all be the Divinely inspired word of The Father, but the typeset, so to speak, is set by you fellas." She held her hands out apologetically. "You have newspapers declaring Herbert Humphrey the election winner, but you expect your typesetting and spell check in something as long as the Bible to be perfect? Let's not forget that you all edited it, too. You know what got left out at Nicea?" She paused and waved her hand dismissively. "Never mind. That's not why I'm here." She smiled and clapped her hands together. "We have business!" She sounded excited with a level of enthusiasm I reserve for Chuck Yeager tweets and *Raiders of the Lost Ark*.

"Okay?" I asked cautiously as my fingers brushed the butt of my pistol.

She put her hands back on her knees and gave me a look that was either disapproving or mock disapproving; I literally couldn't tell which she was shooting at me. "You, really shouldn't have done that favor for Lucifer."

"The dog thing?" Gretchen asked.

Gabrielle smiled. "Oh, Cerberus was such a cute puppy. Does he miss his Auntie Gabby? Wait, how would you know that? Never mind, but yes, the dog thing."

"Why not?" I asked cautiously. "It was a job."

"Honey," Gabrielle said consolingly, "it might as well have been a declaration. You'd do better well not to pick sides. That kind of things makes less cool heads twitchy."

I heard the anger in my voice. I could feel the burning in my gut. The rage pulling at the back of my head. "You bastards forced me onto a side when you killed my goddamned mom and kidnapped my fucking soulmate." I was practically grunting each word and my teeth were bared. I was ready to throw the fuck down.

I felt Gretchen grab my hand and squeeze.

Gabrielle held her hands up, palms out and in a calming voice. "Watch the blasphemy please, but I agree Zadkiel got what was coming to him. Even Michael and Uriel agree on that." She rested her hands back on her knees. "But you can't go around doing favors for one side and not the other. You're safest neutral." She stood slowly and reached out putting her hands on top of Gretchen's and mine. "If neither side thinks you're going to turn for the other, everyone is at their utmost safest. But if you solely do favors and jobs for your Uncle, well, how long is it until we're dealing with *99 Luftballons*?"

I bit my lip.

"What are you offering?" Gretchen said with a forced, but soothing calm.

Gabrielle smiled and sat back demurely. "I have a job for you."

"What's the gig?" I felt my jaw clenching. The fire was there; Gretchen was helping hold it back.

"Well, there are some"—Gabrielle thought for a moment—-"I don't want to call them Devil Worshipers because I like your Uncle. Let's call them demon worshipers because really they're dealing with Berith, not Lucifer. How is he by the way?"

"Good," I half growled.

"He looks like Gary Oldman," Gretchen said cheerily.

"Oh, I love him!" Gabrielle said politely, and excitedly clapped her hands together the way I'd imagine the Queen of England doing for a better than mediocre performance of Shakespeare. "That is so perfect."

"Gabrielle?" I asked, regaining control of my calm. She looked to me with those bright blue eyes. "The job?"

"Oh," she gasped, she continued with a Southern accent thicker than cold molasses. "Dear me, I'm sorry. Well, these demon worshipers have something and they're going to try and summon Berith in three days to give it to him. I don't want Berith to get it." That sounded as complicated as she seemed to think it was simple.

"What do they have?" Agnes asked from her desk where she was dictating the whole conversation. Agnes actually knew shorthand. I didn't even think that was taught anymore. Agnes didn't even question the sanity of what she was hearing. I wished once again that I could afford to give her a raise.

"The Spear of Destiny," Gabrielle said matter-of-factly. "Well, the Spearhead of Destiny anyway. The wood's been replaced a lot."

"Why three days?" Gretchen asked. "Why are they summoning him in three days?"

Gabrielle looked shocked and pointed to the desk calendar. "It's Halloween."

Gretchen's jaw dropped. "They're waiting for Halloween? Why?"

"Well," Gabrielle looked for the right word. "There is no polite way to say it. They're idiots."

"The fuck?" I asked.

"Well," she said calmly, "how smart do you expect demon worshipers to be?"

That struck me as a fair enough point but I didn't want to admit to it. "Okay, we get the Spear tip of Destiny from them." My eyes were narrow, this wasn't rage, this was suspicion. "What do we get?"

"Well, I've thought about that long and hard."

"That's what she said!" gushed Gretchen, excited.

Gabrielle smiled and leaned forward excited. "But I'm open to suggestions."

I looked to Gretchen and leaned close. "What do you think?" I whispered.

"I think," she whispered, "that if this were a movie Reese Witherspoon should play Gabrielle."

"Okay," I whispered. "And that helps with this how?"

"It doesn't," she admitted quietly. "I just thought I should throw it out there. What do you think?"

"It's decent casting," I admitted. Actually, she was spot on.

"Thanks." She smiled and whispered, "and the payment?"

"Swing for the bleachers? See what sticks?" I offered.

"Go for it."

We sat back up and I looked to the archangel. "I and my associates want new cars, cool ones, that will never get speeding tickets or parking tickets, and we don't want to pay taxes."

"Ever," Gretchen added, "We don't want to pay taxes ever." She looked at me and we high-fived. *"Armageddon."*

"I assume you mean yourselves and Agnes?" Gabrielle asked.

"Anyone who helps with the job," I said adamantly. Jammer and Switch were going to love this.

Gabrielle stood and smoothed her skirt. I stood. She held out her hand. "I believe we have an accord." She walked over and Agnes gave her the hat and half cape she'd worn to the office. Once Gabrielle had everything in its proper place she turned and smiled. She walked to the door then paused. "Bruce, is that what you call him? He sends his regards."

She stepped out the door and walked calmly down the hallway. The door slowly closed itself. Gretchen ran over to open the door and look, but the Herald of the Throne was gone.

Chapter Six: Five Types of Strippers

Porn Star Dancing by My Darkest Day

In my experience, I've found that there are five types of girls who become strippers. First are the girls who strip because the economy sucks or it's just the only job she could get. These are the "For Now" girls; the *I'm just doing this FOR NOW, until I can...* Those girls plans are either reasonable or completely bat-shit crazy. I'd met a girl from Howdy's Boobs and Booze Joint who had her MD and was in her fourth year as a Ph.D. candidate already pounding down chapters on her dissertation. She also drove a paid-for BMW and lived in a nicer apartment than her professors. She wasn't stripping any more; last I heard she was putting down two or three hundred thousand a year for some medical company. The contrast to her is Sharky's own C-Section Sapphire, who is still waiting for her shot to be one of the pros on "Dancing with the Stars" even though she had no professional ballroom training; that, or to be a lawyer's mistress.

So, I tried to explain to Switch the updates of my life as succinctly as possible. Jammer and Gretchen kept tag teaming their own colorful commentary, all of which made a jumbled, convoluted tale out of something that—let's be fair—was already complicated. The setting where we were telling the story didn't help things either.

The second is the "In Denial" gals. These are the ones that adamantly call themselves "dancers." A ballerina in a skimpy outfit and a tutu is a dancer until she tears the tutu off and starts twerking, then the ballerina becomes a stripper. There is also probably an amount of body glitter used delineating the line between dancer and stripper, but I'm not sure about the specifics on that one.

Gretchen sat next to me at the table in what should have been a schoolgirl outfit, but the blouse was tied in the middle and the skirt would never pass a school board's dress code; though I do have to admit the pigtails were working for me. The rest of the Sharky's crew ambled about the club fishing for twenties with the lure of lap dances. On the stage, Shallot was going through her routine, which mainly consisted of her making her tits oscillate opposite directions. But when trying to describe to a friend about the craziness of our lives, a strip club was simultaneously the best and worst place to have the conversation.

Switch's eyes were on the girl on stage. "Why Shallot?" he asked.

"Her mom thought it was a gemstone," Gretchen told him over the popping noise of the cracked speakers playing Big and Rich's *Save a Horse Ride a Cowboy*.

Switch and Jammer both looked to Gretchen to gauge her seriousness. Switch's eyes held disbelief; Jammer wasn't so sure.

"Seriously," Gretchen said defensively. "Could anyone make up something that stupid?"

Both Jammer and Switch turned their eyes to me. "What? You think I'm fuckin' feeding her lines now?"

Switch accepted that defense as fair and put his eyes back to the stage. Jammer took a few seconds longer before turning his attention back to his plate of hot wings.

The third type of stripper is the girl who has simply fucked up enough that stripping is the level where they've stopped sinking. She's the girl with too much pride and work ethic to whore, but not enough to do much else. These were your stereotypical young single moms. Some are actually good, loving moms, taking their tips to buy shoes and food and what not for their kids. Some are shitty moms making the others look bad by buying blow with their tips instead of buying school supplies and just making shit harder on the over-worked underpaid teacher.

Gretchen knew a girl at Titanium Lightning named Charity who ran a daycare out of her trailer during the day in the summer for people working first and second shift jobs during the summer. She only grossed about ten bucks a kid over the course of a week, but it let her spend her days with her kid and provided that kid a social structure and ever-ready friends. Whereas Opal at Sharky's had the winning combination of meth teeth and a story about DHS taking her kids away.

Shallot was on stage with a bubble gun at that point, sending up a shower of the soapy floaters and spinning through them as they slowly sank toward the ground. The crappy Sharky's stage lights caught and reflected off the bubbles acting like a slight distraction from the slightly-past-her-prime stripper on stage and actually improving the act.

Jammer cupped his hands over his mouth and hooted and clapped like he'd never seen that trick before. Gretchen laughed.

The fourth type of stripper is the saddest. It's the girl who had something happen in her past that fucked her up to a point that this is all she's good for anymore. These are the girls who were betrayed by a good family friend or teacher or some other disgusting fucked up prick who deserves to be full-body flayed starting with his dick. These are the girls who were beaten by their moms and forced to learn that they're worthless. The girls who one way or another had their value stripped from them, but at least on that stage they find something, even if it's just dollar bills.

I guessed with a name like Shallot she hadn't won the genetic lottery for brains. I wasn't going to assume about her plans or abilities. But what I could see were the perpendicular scars across her wrists. I didn't know her story or her bio, but she was still there kicking her leg awkwardly and not as high as she thought she was able.

Shallot ended her routine and took her bows as she bent to gather up her collection of one-dollar bills off the stage. Switch and Jammer turned their attention back to me and Gretchen and the food on the table. As always the lunch buffet was phenomenal. The fried chicken they had out was better than anything you get in a fast food chicken shop and the biscuits were almost as good as my grandma's before she switched from lard to Crisco.

"I'm calling bullshit," Switch finally said before plunging a fork into a vegetable medley.

"On what?" I asked though I knew I sounded incredulous but couldn't help it.

Switch thought for a moment holding the fork full of veggies halfway between his plate and his mouth. "All of it?" He took the bite.

Jammer scoffed and mumbled around a mouthful of hot wing. "Bullshit. Nick, just show him the sword."

"It doesn't work like that, Jammer." I sighed as the next dancer went up on stage. She was dancing to Christina Agulera's *Candy Man*.

"And how does it work?" Switch asked playing along to see how far I'd push the bullshit. Except this time, it wasn't bullshit.

"I gotta be mad." That was the truth of it.

Jammer leaped to his feet and slammed his hands on the table rattling everything as he screamed. "How many seasons of 'Jersey Shore' and 'Keeping Up with the Kardashians' are there AND 'FIREFLY' GOT CANCELED AFTER ONE SHORT FUCKING SEASON!"

I'd like to say that it didn't work.

Switch's eyes went wide as the burning sword leaped into my hand, the red glowing blade wreathed in fire. I felt the rage. I wanted to put every TV executive's head on spikes. I wanted to punish stupid assholes that watch stupid TV and let good shows die. I wanted to burn the world...

Gretchen put her hand on mine. "It's fine, Nick. We got 'Firefly' on DVD." I looked at her. Her voice cut through the red. The sword dissipated from my grasp.

Skinny Craig the Bartender, as opposed to Fat Craig the Bouncer, called from behind the bar offhandedly and sounding bored. "Keep the fire down will you?" You have to love that about Sharky's at least.

I looked to Gretchen and felt the red fade from the edges of my vision. Then I looked over to Switch. Gretchen smiled to him sweetly. "All of it is bullshit?" Her voice oozed sarcasm and sexuality in equal measure.

Switch sat there a moment staring between Gretchen and me. Gretchen smiled sweetly. "I'm up next." She leaned over and kissed my cheek. "See you after my shift." She waved to Switch and Jammer. "You boys have fun." She glided away with that hip-swaying saunter that could be the cause of glaciers melting.

Switch nodded, then asked with an energy that betrayed a total commitment to the cause. "Okay, no taxes, new car. So what's the plan?"

I couldn't help but smile. "Jammer and I will start beating the bush and see if we can get anything to take flight. We get any leads we'll start chasing them down."

He nodded. "What do you need from me?" That's the thing about buddies you make in wartime. There is no hyperbole about that relationship. You guys are all in, all the time, no matter what. I don't see how regular people can deal with things.

I smirked. "Switch, we need you to do what you do best."

Switch grinned broadly. "Blow shit up?"

Jammer clapped his hot wing saucy hands together and rubbed them with anticipation.

"Not yet," I warned. "But we want to be ready to. I'm talking charges for doors, dynamic wall breaches, water impulse charges, picket charges…"

Jammer chimed in, "And just shit at the ready to fuck up whatever needs fucking up."

I nodded in agreement.

Here's the thing: what we were asking Switch for was stupid illegal. Like lock-us-up-and-throw-away-the-key illegal. Besides all the explosive offensives they'd hit us with they'd throw us under the terrorist bus. With Switch's brown complexion and beard, he'd obviously be an Islamist extremist and Jammer and I would be labeled ultra right-wing nationalists. So asking Switch to be ready to provide whatever type of dynamic answer we might need to an explosive worthy solution wasn't a small thing.

Switch grinned like the Cheshire cat. "I got some stuff in my truck, but I'll need to go to a hardware store. You guys got a place I can work?"

"Go to Secure Cheap Self Storage at the corner of Clifton Street and Parker Avenue. There's a combination lock on locker 325. The combo is 3-5-0-4. In that locker, you'll find a set of keys. At the back of the self storage ,there's an RV. Take that, go where you need to get your work done. But that way you can keep moving if you need to, nap if you want, whatever." Jammer clapped Switch's shoulder. "Welcome to the team."

"Hey," he chided. "I was on the team before the girl was."

Jammer laughed. "Yeah, but you're not as dedicated."

"Oh, yeah?" Switch asked, "How so?"

Jammer gestured to me. "You're not nailing him."

"Hey!" I snapped.

Switch shrugged. "Fair enough." He stood and nodded. "Catch you boys later."

The music changed and I looked up to see Gretchen come out to Eminem's *Lose Yourself*. She knew how to move; she knew how to undress at a sensual pace that didn't involve ripping Velcro.

There is a fifth kind of stripper. The stripper who does it because she actually enjoys it. She enjoys the control over a crowd she can command. She enjoys not having a man's attention but taking his attention. There is a difference. There is a girl who strips because it gives her both pleasure and power.

I don't have to explain which of the five categories Gretchen falls under.

"Where do you want to start?" Jammer asked, not even pretending to not be watching my soulmate.

"I'm open." My eyes were locked on her, too.

"I have an idea," Jammer suggested, "but you are not going to like it."

"Try me."

"We should check out the Akashic Record," he said slowly as Gretchen turned her back to the crowd while working her hips.

"Why would I not like that? Makes sense from what you've said." I watched Gretchen lose the skirt. The thong did not look comfortable.

"Digging through the Akashic Record isn't like Wikipedia, bro. You don't put a search in the search bar and go," Jammer explained as if he were telling a kid 'Don't touch a stove, idiot!' "We need someone good with computers..."

"No." I knew where he was going.

"... someone who knows how to navigate it with the loose parameters we can give them..."

"No." I didn't like where he was going with this.

"... someone who can give us the info fast."

"I'd rather fucking die choking on a goddamn dick." I told it plainly and adamantly and as honest as I could.

Jammer sounded genuinely consoling as he said the one thing I didn't want to hear. "We need to go the Grand Vizier Megatron Terabyte the Cyber Samurai."

Chapter Seven: Grand Vizier Megatron Terabyte the Cyber Samurai

Turning Japanese by The Vapors

Walking into the place, you really felt like you understood what the guy was talking about when he said: "I think I'm turning Japanese, I think I'm turning Japanese, I really think so." Behind the heavy industrial door there was one of those sliding paper panel doors that you'd imagine finding in a rokua; but to be fair, odds are you've never been to Japan either so it's all ultimately guesswork. Behind that sliding door, there were the mats, the wood paneling, sliding paper doors, hanging paper lanterns, little chubby Buddha incense burner, rack to put your shoes, and several kimono hanging on a rack. It was like a douchebag Japanophile ejaculated everywhere.

Without missing a beat the indefatigable Jammer walked over and kicked his shoes onto the rack and started undressing. He tried taking his button-up shirt and T-shirt off at the same time, getting it caught over his head like he was in a fight with another hockey player, but it was just him. I chuckled as he got it over his head and was tugged it down his arms.

"What?" He asked as he dropped the shirts instead of hanging them. He fumbled with his belt and dropped his trousers right then and there. I averted my eyes not because I hadn't seen Jammer's junk before, but because I'd seen it more times than I'd ever wanted to. I knew if I could go the rest of my life without ever seeing Jammer's junk again I'd have still seen it too many times. "What, dude?" he said, arms held out wide and modesty as foreign a concept as mayonnaise on French fries, or eating snails.

"Just," I sighed, easier to fight the tide in the Bay of Fundy. "Just put the fuckin' kimono on." He put on a kimono that I was positive belonged to a woman. It was so short I was surprised I couldn't see the end of his cock dangling, but maybe it was the angle I was standing.

"Okay, dude, what are you waiting for?" Jammer asked as he untied and then retired the obi.

"I'm not doing it," I said flatly.

He sighed. "Dude, you know the rules."

"Fuck the fucking goat-fucked rules," I growled. I could feel the rage tugging at the back of my mind. I knew that would be a problem going there but it's different when it's not abstract but an actual reality. I was willing to bet all this Japanese paper bullshit would burn...

I shook my head and made eye contact with Jammer. He spoke knowing and calmly. "It's going to be okay, this is just the quickest way to get what we need."

I angrily bent down and untied my Chucks, tugging of one then the next. I threw my shoes, trying to knock over the rack. I was not successful but it felt gratifying nonetheless. I got out of my suit jacket, shoulder rig, and shirt. Unlike Jammer, I got the kimono around me before reaching under it to drop my slacks. I hung the pants, shirt, shoulder rig and jacket on one hanger. I was pleased to see the cheap plastic hanger sag under the weight of the pistol and mags. Fuck that coat hanger.

Jammer and I stepped up to the next sliding door. It opened automatically and we walked down a short hallway. I knew there was enough copper and current behind the pseudo-Japanese paneling to fuck with any bugs or other recording devices. That was the point anyway.

The door was at the end of the hallway, and there to greet us was the most annoying person on the planet. She was easily six-foot-one and would be considered a plus-sized model but no one in the real world would call her fat; full maybe, but not fat. She had well kept topiary-like black hair that I knew for a fact to be a wig. Her face was made up to be the perfect representation of a geisha, except not a real geisha, but the representation of a geisha as imagined by an idiot White Anglo Saxon Protestant. She wore a black and yellow karate gi that I literally think was a costume from the original *Karate Kid* movie from the Cobra Ki dojo. In her belt she had stuffed a sheathed katana, but instead of a real katana each with each of the eight parts of the whole made by a master, it was a definite knockoff katana bought in a wannabe Asian junk shop in a mall. Her toes were each painted pick with an individual "Hello Kitty" on them.

I've never punched a woman in the face, but the blood leaking from a broken nose would have looked awesome across her annoying white-caked face. I knew I didn't mean that. But sometimes we all think things we don't mean. Parents think horrible things about their kids when they want them to shut up, even if only for a second. People want, even if only for a second, the people in the car causing the traffic jam to die. I didn't want her to get her nose broken, not really. Did I? Sometimes with the sword, it was hard to tell.

"Jammer, it's a pleasure as always," she said demurely with a pseudo-Asian accent that was completely faked.

"Grand Vizier Megatron Terabyte." Jammer bowed low. "It's an honor to stand in the presence of the Cyber Samurai."

She bowed and I felt the urge to kick her in her face as she did. I don't like a lot of people. I thought of the hajj back in the war that tried to kill me, I disliked them. I don't think I've ever hated anyone. But if that wacky bitch were on fire I wouldn't piss on her to put it out.

She turned her sickly blue eyes on me. "Nick."

"Yeah…" I said slowly. "I need some fuckin' info." I was proud of myself. I wasn't yelling, I wasn't growling, I wasn't gritting my teeth… hard anyway.

"Nick." Her annoying voice sound annoyed. "If you don't respect me…"

"Define respect?" I asked, interrupting. "I mean, do you mean skills? I respect your skills or else I wouldn't be wearing this stupid shit." I gestured at the kimono, which was faux silk and made in China. "Respect you as a person? Fuck no."

"I don't get what you hate about me." She sounded exasperated. "We've not clicked, I'll agree with that." That seemed an understatement to me. "But I think if you spent more time with me…"

"Let me stop you there." I held my hand out. "You ever see *Kickboxer*?"

She shook her head no and her wig shifted as she did. She reached up to adjust it as I continued.

"So Van Damme has to wrap his hands in cloth, then dip them in glue, then dip them in broken glass. I'd rather do that, then punch myself in the dick than spend an extra fucking second with you that I don't have to."

"Why?" She sounded hurt, and I found her so annoying I didn't care.

I heard Jammer sucking in air next to me, which I'm pretty sure was him psychically trying to send me the message, *Please keep your fucking suck shut, bro.*

I lowered my head and looked up at her through my eyebrows. "What's your name?"

Her mouth tightened and her insanely plucked eyebrows arched angrily. "I am the Grand Vizier…"

"That's Islamic, not Japanese."

"Megatron…" she seethed, but pressed on.

"A Decepticon created by Hasbro."

"Terabyte the Cyber Samurai!"

Apparently, me questioning her bullshit made her as mad as her very existence made me.

"You really want to do this?" I asked coldly.

She nodded in the affirmative.

"You're not," I said slowly. "Japanese, you're not even part Japanese. I've seen you without the goddamn wig and makeup. You have..." I looked to Jammer, confused. "You know, not red hair not blonde hair?"

"Strawberry blonde?" he offered helpfully.

"Yeah, you have strawberry blonde hair and you're a freaking pale as an agoraphobic vampire. And your name..." I was getting pissed; I didn't want to come here even if she was good at what she did. "Your name..." I growled. "Is fucking Megan Tara Meyer. You literally have the whitest name on the fucking planet and that's coming from a guy named goddamned Nick! You want to know how my parents came up with my name. *Oh, I'm shaving, oh shit, I know what to name the boy!* Your parents had to have been white freaking supremacists because they chose to give you a goddamned name that would never leave any doubt in anyone's mind of your racial fucking white girl purity!"

Jammer punched me in the face, pretty hard.

My head snapped back but I didn't go down. Since the Fiery Sword started to manifest I'd gotten tougher. I could hit a lot harder, and I could take a hit. Jammer and I had been testing it. I was good for five hard face punches before I started really feeling them. So it didn't hurt, but it got my attention and seemed to please the collection of offensive stereotypes at the end of the hall.

"Damnit, Megatron, you remember what we did for you? We're calling in the marker." Jammer sounded angry but it snapped both her back and me to reality.

"What *we* did for her?" I asked. I remembered what I did for her; I didn't know what the hell Jammer was thinking he did.

"Yeah, scumbag, we." Jammer punched me in the face again. She laughed as it happened and didn't do anything to garner any sympathy or empathy for her from me.

"What did we do?" I asked confused as I reached up and rubbed my jaw.

"You," Jammer stabbed my chest with his finger, "went as her date to her ten-year high school reunion." He turned and pointed angrily to her and snapped. "He also had dinner with you and your parents telling them he's never been happier and things were going great in order to get them off your ass about your dating life."

"Yeah, but..." She started but stopped as I cut her off.

"What the fuck did you do? We, my ass."

He looked to me and spoke in a slow, staccato manner that was sharp enough to Ginsu a tin can. "I arranged it."

I wanted to make the argument that that was not an equitable division of labor. But this wasn't the place to have that conversation. I looked up to Megan Tara Meyer; because I refused to call her The Grand Vizier Megatron Terabyte the Cyber Samurai.

"You do this," I said slowly and as calmly as I could, "and we're square."

She sat and nearly spat. "I was a pleasure on both occasions."

"A pleasure?" I asked. "Maybe if you realized no one gives a shit about your shippy Naruto fan-fucking-fiction you could have found your own fucking date to your own fucking reunion."

"Oh yeah, is that how you got a date to your reunion?" She put her hand on her hip shifting the katana and causing the end to knock something over behind her that I couldn't see, but the crash was audible and obvious. To her credit she ignored it.

"Joke's on you, bitch. I didn't go to my reunion. High school is a prison. You have to be there but when you're out why the fuck would you want to go back?" I laughed.

"Didn't you have friends?" she asked curiously.

"Yeah, and the people that I give enough of a fuck to keep up with I make the occasional half-ass effort to get in touch with once every few years."

I get that that made me sound like a dick, and I probably was, but people drift apart. Denying it was naive, and accepting it was a dick move; so you're fucked either way. Life goes on after high school. Plus why would I want to go back? I hated most of those dickbags when I had to see them every day and those insipid pieces of shit left so much of an influence on me I can't even fucking remember them. The folks I can remember matter, but I didn't need a reunion to see or shoot the occasional message to; the rest, fuck them.

She chewed her lower lip for a few moments angrily. "My Naruto fanfic is phenomenal."

"Sure," I assure her without adding, *and I'm sure it'll get you a Nebula Award in the next year or so, next stop: Pulitzer time!*

I think Jammer sensed the sarcastic remark being bitten back and he nodded to me like the proud mentor in the movie whose student just made the game-winning play; the mentor who nods slowly from the back of the crowd as the ineffectual parents cheer like the glory is theirs.

"What," she asked slowly, "exactly do you need?"

Jammer turned to face her and held his hands out like it was the simplest request in the world. "We just need you to run some searches on the Akashic Network."

Her eyes went wide in surprise. "Oh, wow..."

Chapter Eight: You Don't Have to Like Someone to Respect His or Her Abilities

Ooh La La by The Faces

I hated her, but even I had to admit she had a great looking setup, even if she ruined it with her bullshit. You can despise someone as a person but still respect his or her abilities. At her high school reunion, everyone had called her "Tara" so that's what I called her. Her setup was impressive and reminded me of an intel center in a movie. On one wall she had nine large flat-screen monitors playing CNN, MSNBC, FOX News, CSPAN, four local stations that would possibly shift to breaking news if something noteworthy happened. The last monitor was playing Naruto.

On the opposite wall from the news was another wall of monitors. These were all security feeds covering the nondescript industrial park building she occupied. The wall between those two was another wall of nine large flat-screen monitors. Most of those divided into quarter screens. In front of this was a deep half-moon desk with smaller monitors and several keyboards, computer mice and other assorted touch pads and tablets. What there weren't in the room were computers themselves. She must have kept them in another, heavily air-conditioned room.

She plopped down in a large, plush, sci-fi looking chair and spun to face Jammer and I. In the background were the pulsing techno beats of some unrecognizable Japanese pop group. She reached down and pulled her sheathed katana from her belt because it poked awkwardly as she wiggled in the chair and tried to get comfortable. There were no other chairs in the room and I wouldn't have sat had there been. I didn't want to put up with Tara's idiotic infantile bullshit longer than I had to. Jammer found a coffee pot and a stack of disposable cups and decided to help himself.

"Okay, dickbags," Tara asked as she steepled her fingers in front of her in her best—albeit still shitty—impression of a Bond villain. "What are you looking for on the Akashic Network?"

"We're looking for any local hits on the Spear of Destiny," I told her. And yes I felt stupid asking it, but that was the world we found ourselves living in, wasn't it?

She turned and began typing. One of the large monitors on the wall shifted then the rest changed as well. They all contained a large, interconnected three-dimensional web connecting multiple clusters of data. Everything affected everything else. Every time she electronically tugged on a threat the entire web shifted. To put it technically, it looked complicated as fuck.

She caught my confusion out of the corner of her eye. "What do you think?"

"It makes me miss Ask Jeeves," I admitted as I watched the entire web undulate.

She giggled in that fake way people do when they are trying to be cute, but it wasn't an honest giggle and that brought the angry tug at the back of my mind. "That's cute," she said lightly with another disingenuous giggle.

"Keep it in your pants, Tara," I half growled. "I got an awesome goddamned girlfriend."

That caused her to slump in her seat. Tara's dumbassery she called "character" made me really appreciate Gretchen.

"Okay," she said without commitment or taking her focus from the monitors. "Do you want print outs or do you want me to talk you through it?"

"Both," answered Jammer as he slurped his coffee.

"You want me to start at the beginning?" She began opening screens on multiple monitors.

"Start with traffic in the last seventy-two hours." I really didn't want to have it go back further than that. As useful as historical information might be, that was something we could go through later. What we needed now were leads; the more solid the better.

She started some kind of search protocol and let it run. "Jammer?" she asked as she scrolled through multiple screens of information. "Can you be a doll and bring me a refill?" She took the stylus and tapped her empty coffee mug which was covered in anime characters, none of which I recognized. Jammer brought over the coffee pot and poured a mug with all the deft skill of an experienced, haggard yet nonplused waitress.

"Cream or sugar?" he asked politely.

"Two cubes, please." That answer from Tara was reflexive; she really wasn't paying attention to us. Her focus was somehow simultaneously on multiple monitors at once. You don't have to like someone to respect his or her abilities. She was good at what she did, but I'd put a bullet in my fucking brainpan before I'd call her a damned Cyber Samurai.

"Someone," she somehow said with six slow syllables, "boosted it two days ago. It was done here, local." She turned her attention to another monitor. "And there is going to be an auction for it day after tomorrow. Right now, people are bidding for seats to the auction itself. So they're looking at a profit from that alone."

Jammer used a pair of tongs to lift two sugar cubes from the small brown bowl and started across the room with them. He got about halfway before he dropped them. He looked at them, the look on his face giving away the mental debate about the five-second rule before he turned back to the brown bowl of sugar cubes to try again.

Tara picked up the mug and sipped the sugarless coffee without seeming to taste it at all.

"Can you get me a list of bidders?" I stared at the monitors trying to find where she was getting the info and came up drier than Death Valley in whatever the opposite of monsoon season would be.

"Working on it now." Her voice was distant almost like it was a preprogrammed response in an automated system. Tara was easier to not want to pop in the gob while she was working. "Want me to cross-reference the list with anything to help narrow the parameters to a tighter focus?"

"Berith," I told her, remembering the conversation with Gabrielle. "Cross-reference them with Berith."

Jammer lifted another two sugar cubes. He started walking back toward Tara and her coffee mug. He held his hand under the tongs as he slowly walked heel to toe, heel to toe. He got three-quarters of the way before losing the sugar cubes. He managed to catch one but one hit the floor. The cube that Jammer caught he managed to crush. "Son of a bitch!"

"Cross-referencing with Berith," Tara said as she scrolled through more data. "There is actually a decent amount of *infernal* and *celestial* activity." She laughed.

"What?" I asked curiously.

"I mean, infernal and celestial." She held her stomach and laughed. "Come on, it's idiotic." She pointed to one screen. "Look at this. Saying the archangel Gabriel was in town this morning." She chuckled and sipped more sugarless coffee. "Says here, the archangel Zadkiel was killed last week!" Had it been a damn week already? Holy shit.

"I mean," she sipped the coffee and laughed, "who makes this shit up?" She wiped her eyes smearing the garish makeup.

"Any hits on Berith?" I wanted to change the subject before she really started looking at things.

"As archangels go Zadkiel is supposed to be a good one." She commented calmly as she kept looking down the data flow. "Stopped Abraham from killing Isaac."

"Tara," I said a little too harshly, but she looked up from the screens to me. "Back on task, Tara," I said calmly.

She huffed and thankfully dropped that window. "I've gotten a hit on the auction and a Baalberith connection."

I leaned close, completely unaware of what the fuck I was looking at. "What do we have?"

"Eric Travis," she said as she squinted at the screen.

"Okay," I said slowly. "Anything more than that? Who the fuck is Eric Travis?"

"A douchebag from the sound of it," Jammer muttered as he dropped the sugar cubes. He caught them, but they crushed to powder in his palm as he caught them. "MOTHER FUCKER!"

Tara went back to typing and opened up some more windows. "Eric Travis, a professor over at the university. He does work with the English department, studied overseas."

"Define overseas?" Jammer asked. To be fair overseas could be Hawaii.

"England and France," she answered quickly after scanning the data stream. "Then he taught in Egypt and ended up on a few digs."

"You mean in a few digs?" Jammer asked carrying the whole bowl of sugar cubed.

Tara took another sip of her coffee and sat the mug down and enlarged a window. "No, I mean archeological stuff. Possible links to antiquities theft, not official but there are some shady dudes in Cyprus that wouldn't mind grilling his nuts."

"Has he won a bid spot?" I asked.

"Yep, he was the first. "

"What's his connection to Berith?" I still couldn't make heads or tails to any of the shit she was looking at.

"He's written some papers about how Baalberith is just some kind of Id representation blah blah blah." She twisted her fingers over and over. She then reached up under the wig to scratch.

I nodded. "Anything on the seller?"

She typed some more. "Rodion Romanovich Raskolnikov."

I felt my brow furrow. "Fuck?'

Jammer looked down into Tara's empty coffee mug as the sound of *tink tink* hit his ears as the cubes hit the bottom of the empty cubes. "Son of a bitch..." he muttered and walked the bowl of cubes back to the table with the coffee machine.

She had a confused look. "Something's not right about that but I don't know what it is..."

"It's Fyodor Dostoyevsky," I said quietly.

She looked up to me confused, and for a moment her and Jammer shared the look. "How the fuck do you know that?" Jammer asked. Then followed with "Who is Theodor Dusty-eye-ski."

"Rodion Romanovich Raskolnikov is the main character in *Crime and Punishment*." I pushed on; I wasn't falling into a pronunciation hole with Jammer.

"What are you saying?" Tara asked.

"It's a pseudonym. A fake fucking name." I thought for a moment then looked to Tara. "The auction is cash in hand right?"

She checked then nodded. "Yes, it is. Why?"

I scratched the top of my head. "It's a setup."

"What are you thinking, Nick?" Jammer asked, crossing back to us.

"Travis has the Spear, and he's setting up the auction, getting money for people to show up. Then it's gonna go one of two ways. He's gonna sell it, or he's gonna roll everyone."

"How much could it be worth?" Jammer asked. "I mean, it's a fucking spear."

"Not according to all this," said Tara as she pulled up a new window.

"What do you mean?" Jammer asked.

"So Cain killed Abel, right?" she started with her Socratic lecture. "Well, apparently, according to this stuff anyway, Cain killed Able with a lump of iron. That iron got turned into the Spear. Goliath carried the Spear before David killed him then David took it. Saint George carried it when he killed the dragon. All kinds of crazy shit like that. Even besides poking Christ to make sure he was dead on the cross."

"So you're saying it's literally the first weapon?" Jammer asked slightly slack-jawed.

I looked down at my right hand and felt the burning itch. I felt the slight tug at the back of my mind. Not anger pulling at me but righteous pride. There is something fucking terrible about righteousness. "Not the first weapon," I muttered.

Jammer locked understanding eyes with me.

"Print all this shit out, Tara," I muttered before adding, "Thanks."

"How much do you want?" she asked as she started accessing her printers.

"All of it."

"That's going to be a couple reams of paper and who knows how much toner," she complained.

"Slash and burn a fucking forest for all I care," I grunted. I had a lead. I had work to do.

Chapter Nine: Betty or Veronica?

Straight to Hell by Drivin' and Cryin'

The song goes "I'm goin' straight to Hell, just like my momma said." A lot of the song might not have applied to me but the chorus certainly did.

We left Tara's place with several binders full out printouts. Even I admitted that it was good of her to provide the binders and the canvas grocery bags to easily carry them in. Tara's day job was checking, securing, and testing corporate firewalls. I'm also pretty sure that companies that didn't hire her services suffered for it: twenty-first-century protection racket. Maybe the future of organized crime was loner white girls who wished they were Japanese. To be honest Tara could have been a poster girl for the movement to get girls into STEM fields, except for the fact that she was bat-shit crazy and as weird as dolls in horror movies.

I checked my phone after we got out of Tara's Faraday trap and saw I had a text. I really didn't want to answer it but I did.

Jammer and I headed our separate directions to double our productivity. There was a collection of dealers, pimps, and other shady characters Jammer knew who he would ask about Eric Travis, who I was certain was Rodion Romanovich Raskolnikov. I put in a call to a desk sergeant at the Fifth Precinct and reminded him of a favor I did for him in the past and then asked if he could help me out with information on Dr. Eric Travis with a Ph.D. in English Bullshit. The desk sergeant asked if I could give him a couple of hours. I told him to take his time but definitely implied to not take too fucking much time.

I walked down the road with hands stuffed in my pockets before reaching into the inside right pocket of the jacket and pulled out my flask. I unscrewed the cap and took a long slug of 18-year-old Macallan from the neck before screwing the top back and sliding it home in my pocket. Some things you just need some liquid help to steel yourself for.

At that point, I'd been thinking a lot about the Drivin' N' Cryin' song *Straight to Hell*. Even back before I learned my mom had been the twenty-third demon kicked out of Heaven and onto her ass, bits of that song had resonated with me. In retrospect, she'd told me, "You're going to go straight to Hell," quite a bit as I got older. Particularly after I'd joined the Army and given up on my family's bullshit. It was like vinyl siding on a rotted frame; looked good on the outside but the whole thing was rotted.

On the outside, my old man had seemed bright and reasonable. Deep down he was an authoritative prick who couldn't handle the fact that I eventually saw through the bullshit and decided to question it. Mom's failing was she backed him to the hilt, without question and without complaint enough to do anything. Mom was the perfect "company man." My brother was a piece of shit and they enabled it. Once my mom called me at two in the morning because dad was away and my brother had gotten pulled over for a DUI. She asked me what to do. I told her to leave him in jail; maybe it'd do him some good to stew. But they got him out. After his divorce, he lived rent-free, basically jobless, and they raised his kids for him.

Do you know what you wouldn't find had you looked at my brother's bank statements for that decade? A fucking pair of kid's shoes, but you would find plenty of cigarettes. It was all done in the name of the kids, like that was some holy fucking writ. But somehow carrying him was part of the fucking deal. I never bitched about that too voraciously, because it was in-house.

I made my break with my folks when they subsidized his new fiancée's divorce. They ignored the fact that they got together during an affair. Ignored the fact that she was the wife of a good friend of mine. Ignored the fact that he was a good goddamned father whose biggest mistake was sticking his dick into a wacked out crazy bitch. He put himself thirty grand in debt fighting for his kids and still ended up with the biggest shit sandwich of custody deals. The girls spent one year with their mom and one year with him. My parents did that. My parents fucked a good man out of his kids all for the sake of my shithead brother. That's why I walked.

Mom had told me, "You're going to go straight to Hell." She must have known what she was talking about. That said, I was certain they were going to burn in a hotter part of Hell than me. Uncle Lew liked me.

So the fact that I was standing in the food court of a mall at that moment was phenomenally fucking gracious on my part. I was digging my plastic fork into a Cinnabon when I heard his voice behind me.

"I heard you have a girlfriend now." I heard the voice and saw my brother standing there.

I'm goin straight to Hell, just like my momma said. I'm goin' straight to Hell.

"Okay," I said around the bite of deliciousness, without any commitment to the statement. To be honest it was better than answering *I've murdered too many people on her behalf for her to be just my girlfriend.*

The big problem with my brother was, he was a chameleon. If you threw him in a room with a bunch of thug bikers whose great virtue was loyalty to the club, within the hour he'd be professing his regret that he hadn't been given the opportunity to die for the club.

If you tossed him in a pit of feminists within moments he'd be lamenting the oppression his penis had caused womanhood. Launch him into a convention of English professors and he'd be seeing sex and death in everything. See, he wasn't a person; he was a mirror of whomever he was around.

He didn't know me; he hadn't known me for years. So his act—and it was an act whether he realized it or not—was a character that didn't fit the reality of the man in front of him.

He smiled—most people saw him as a charming guy—and he gave me the feel of sticking my hand in the water you boiled hotdogs in.

"So," he began as he moved in for a hug. I got my cinnamon roll out of the way as he got his arms around me. I gave him three pats on the back and wished he'd fucking learn how to man-hug. "Is she a Betty or Veronica?"

I wanted to punch him in his fucking face and give him an honest broken nose as opposed to the way he broke it the first time. He yanked a door open too hard and fast when he was stoned and stopped it with his sniffer.

I could smell the cigarettes on him and wondered again how many time's he'd quit. I'd given up counting. I was sure he believed the next one would be the last time for real. I finally broke the hug and stabbed at a bit of cinnamon roll with my black plastic fork. "Whaddaya want?" *Whatdoya* came out as one word.

He smiled with amphibian charm. "Just to see how you were doing. Haven't seen you since the funeral."

Yes, it'd been a little more than a week or so since mom's funeral; before that, it'd been three years since I'd seen him.

I took a bite of cinnamon roll and savored it before looking to him and swallowing.

"Well I'm on the clock for a case so if that's all this is I gotta go."

I turned and started striding away. Fuck him and his trying to play good brother to try to butter me up bullshit. I saw through him like a clear sliding glass door people walk into.

"Well, there is something." He jogged to keep up.

"No shit." I dropped the empty Cinnabon container in a trashcan. "Spit it out. I got shit to do."

"Look," he said as reasonable as he could, "we're brothers we…"

"That's fucking debatable. Just get to the fucking point. There ain't no reason this should last longer than two minutes."

"Before dad died he was going to change the will to set up college funds for the kids. After he died mom never got around to it."

So this was about money? That made sense. I glanced over to him. "How fucking much did they leave me?" So that's why he was there.

His face contorted. He'd always thought he was a good actor, but right now you couldn't tell it. And all his shithead community theater fun really paid dividends. "Well, it's complicated…"

"Make it fucking simple." I felt a smirk tug at my mouth. "Explain it so you can understand it and I should be fine on the comprehending."

He tried to not look angry. You could see him telling himself he needed me agreeable. That felt good. That felt like power. The guy with nothing to lose and wants nothing is the perfect foil for a needy little bitch that has nothing to bargain with but sentimentality. Sentimentality versus spiteful "not give a fuck," the battle of the century, lopsided though.

"Half," he finally said.

I'm goin straight to Hell, just like my momma said. I'm goin' straight to Hell.

I laughed. He didn't like it and that made me laugh more.

So my parents' big reconciliation plan had been to show that they loved their sons evenly with the writing of their last will and testament. That was fucking rich. They spent over a decade up and carrying my shithead brother in the name of the kids. They spent so much time crammed up their grandkids' asses they pretty much let every other relationship suffer. My mom had spent a decade asking me, "When are you going to come visit?"

I finally got to the point where my answer was "When the hell are you?" The only reason they ever saw me is because I came to them, or I was moving and guilted them into helping me load and unload a truck. It's not a relationship if one party does all the fucking legwork and the other simply phones it the fuck in. Know what it is when one person does all the fucking work and others get to reap the rewards of it? It's basically fucking slavery.

The grandkids weren't grandkids; they were crutches. They were validation for every fucking mistake they made with my shithead brother and to a lesser extent me. Maybe the fact that the kids were definitely above average validated it on the back end. But with their parents, my nieces and nephews didn't win the genetic lottery.

If someone washes, drives, and takes care of one car, and leaves the other on blocks and expects it to run when needed, someone doesn't love the cars equally.

I'd always known my folks had loved my brother more. I was the loner asshole that played Dungeons & Dragons and camped and preferred being alone. He was the one you could brag about back in the day. But deeper than that, he was the one that NEEDED love more than me; squeaky wheel and all.

Leaving me half to show that they really did love us equal. *See, here's tangible monetary proof of your equality so forget about time and effort. Now that we're dead don't carry that ire around anymore, Nick.*

Fuck you.

I laughed in his face and started walking off.

"Nick, what are you going to do?"

I smirked as I turned back to him and stuffed my hands in my pockets. "What's it to you?"

"Nick, the kids..."

"The kids what? How about this: I sign all of it over to you. What's the guarantee the kids ever see it? How do I know it won't go to douchebag guitars, or whatever bills you got, or to whatever new drug you're only experimenting with? I fucking don't."

It looked like he was going to angry cry. That would be attractive.

I cut him off before he could say anything. "I won't say I trust you as far as I could throw you, because honestly, I know I can throw you farther."

I stepped to him and planted two fingers in his chest. I felt the anger pulling at the back of my mind and those two fingers knocked him on his ass. I glared down at him. "I'll make this clear. Lose my number. Don't Ever Call On Me Again. And I swear you ever show up on my doorstep I'll kill you and make it look like you came at me so all I did was done in self-fucking-defense." My voice went somber and quivered with regretful emotion. *"Your Honor, I used the minimum amount of force necessary to subdue the situation. He just wouldn't stop, he wouldn't stop. Why wouldn't he just stop?"*

He wasn't smart enough to know how serious I was, for there wasn't any fear in his eyes. But there fucking should have been. I turned and left him there.

I'm goin straight to Hell, just like my momma said. I'm goin' straight to Hell.

You know what my parents' biggest mistake was? Forgetting that their sons were different men. For not realizing that while one son was a bitch, the other was a hard bastard.

I called Phil the Destroyer and explained the situation to him. He referred me to a lawyer that dealt with estate law. I told that guy what I wanted. The money to go in a trust to fund the six kids' college, but under no circumstances was my brother to ever get a goddamned finger on it. If anything was left over after their educations were done was to be split evenly and donated to the American Civil Liberties Union in the name of the NRA and the National Rifle Association in the name of the ACLU. I knew that would confuse the fuck out of people.

I didn't want their goddamned apologies or their fucking apology money, living or dead.

I headed back toward Sharky's where I was going to meet up with Gretchen. Her shift would be done by the time I got there.

Is she a Betty or Veronica?

Who the fuck would pick Betty Cooper over Veronica Lodge?

Chapter Ten: Experiencing People Outside Their Common Paradigm

The Wall by Pink Floyd

I was on my way back to Sharky's when I got a call from the desk sergeant. He sounded twitchy, but he was always twitchy. It was like doing a favor, giving confidential files to a private investigator because of a combination of owing him a favor and the P.I. having dirt on you was really something you could get in trouble for. I met him in a parking structure down the road from the precinct. Real Woodward and Bernstein shit.

He stood in the shadows and asked in a muffled voice, "Were you followed?"

I stuffed my hands into my suit pockets. "Well, if I was followed isn't it a little late to be worried about it now? I mean, we're both here, not like whoever would have followed me doesn't have eyes on both of us right now. So if I were followed you're fucked anyway.

So really were you asking 'cause you were curious or because it's one of those asinine things people in movies ask?"

He started jerking his head left and right looking for the mysterious "they" or "them" who might be after him. Unless he was into some shadier shit than banging the occasional hooker behind dumpsters he really didn't need to worry.

"Jesus Christ," I muttered. "You're fucking fine, I wasn't followed."

He held out a manila envelope. "That's what you asked for and I mean all of it. So don't go thinking I'm holding out on you or that I didn't get everything and you want me to do more; because there's nothing more to do. Okay?"

I shook my head as I took the envelope. "Fuck, man, when was the last time you went to the doctor?"

He looked at me confused. "What do you mean?"

"You seriously fucking need to up your fucking dosage of whatever blood pressure medication you're supposed to be on." I looked him over, as he was pale and sweating. "Does your left arm hurt?"

He looked confused but shook his head no. "No, why?"

"No reason." I smirked and walked off with the envelope leaving him there in his paranoia before he could have a heart attack and I had to get him to the hospital. That would have fucked with my plans for the rest of the day.

I took a hit from the flask and opened the envelope to find what the cops had on Dr. Eric Travis Ph.D. A couple of things struck me right off the bat. First, never trust someone with two first names; at best they're shady, at worse they're a seriously fucked up individual. So, I figured at best this guy was a douchebag perv who was trying to stick his wang into his students and at worst he was a demon-worshiping tool who was going to roll a bunch of religious and demonic tool bags with a scam using the Spear of Destiny as bait. Either way, he didn't strike me as a guy I'd want to have a beer with.

The second thing I noticed was he was employed at the university. So I hopped a bus and rode there, scanning through the police files on the way. As I got off the bus I folded up the envelope and slid it into one of my pockets. From there it took me about an hour to find his car in one of the parking lots. Pretending to tie my shoe I took a burner phone out of my pocket. It had an adhesive strip on the back; I just had to pull off the tab and then stuck it up under the car. Then I hit the power button and walked off.

So twenty years ago maybe planting bugs and tracking devices was probably a specialized thing. But nowadays with burner phones, command adhesive strips and "Find My Lost Fucking Phone apps" tracking people had become idiotically easy and open for amateurs. In terms of electronically tracking people, I was still amateur enough to still compete in the Olympics; at least until they put Scotch on the banned substance list.

I asked some twenty-year-old shithead—he had a waxed and curled mustache who probably had a bright future as a barista after he spent six years and a hundred thousand dollars getting a gender economy degree—where to find Edwards Hall. As big a shit head as I could be, at least my student loans were paid off, and as much as I enjoyed my poli-sci degree, I do think my life might have been better had I become a carpenter. Curly-Mustache McVirgin pointed me toward Edwards Hall where the English department was stashed away.

Walking there I saw a medium height blonde girl with neon green streaks in her hair. For a second I thought she was mean-mugging me, and then I realized she was trying to figure out where she knew me from. That made me wonder if I should recognize her. She wore a vintage (meaning old) Def Leppard *Pyromania* tour T-shirt and tight jeans.

"Nick?" she asked cautiously.

My eyes narrowed a bit. "Yeah?"

She smiled and gave me a hug; it was pleasant, but awkward, as I had no fucking idea who had just wrapped her arms around me.

"It's so good to see you. What are you doing here?" she asked happily.

I slowly shook my head and decided to give it the honest approach instead of faking the funk. "Look, I'm sorry, but I'm not placing you right now."

She laughed then looked around and made sure no one was overtly looking. Then she lifted the front of the Def Leppard shirt. I saw the bra underneath holding her D-cups up and together. The bra was the same neon green as the streaks in her hair. "Oh," I said, "Hey, Andie, how are you doing?"

She laughed good-natured and lowered the shirt smoothing it out. "I'm good. How's Gretchen?"

Andie was one of the girls who worked the circuit between the Titanium Lightning Club and Howdy's Boobs and Booze Club. I just didn't recognize her in the unfamiliar new context. "She's good, doing a shift at Sharky's right now. What are you doing here?"

She held shook the backpack on her shoulder. "Just got done with class. I got one more, then I'm off to work. What are you doing here?"

"Work thing." Now I decided to play it vague.

"Ah." She smiled brightly like an amateur who had spent her life watching James Bond movies finding out there was a covert op going on right around her.

"What are you studying?" I asked, trying to change the subject. Well, actually I was changing the subject, I wasn't trying; what I was hoping is she'd take the bait.

"Postmodern Gender Studies." She smiled.

"Oh." I nodded. "Cool."

She threw her head back and laughed. "I'm kidding, I'm studying biochemistry."

I laughed because she'd gotten me for a second so she deserved it.

"So where are you headed?" she asked.

"Edwards Hall."

"Oh, you don't want to go that way, it'll take you to the front and it'll be packed right now with people not understanding right-of-way through doors. I'll take you around back."

I followed her as she took me down another sidewalk around the building to a set of double doors down at the back of the building. There were couple people milling about but nothing I'd describe as a "crowd."

She smiled. "Here you go."

"Thanks," I said with a half-grin. "I'll tell Gretchen you said hi."

"You better!" She laughed before giving me a hug and sauntered away. You could tell several of the guys' eyes were following her as she glided down the sidewalk. I half-debated saying something, and then decided she was a big girl and could take care of herself. But that's the world we live in. Say something and you are a misogynist who doesn't think she can take care of herself. Don't say something and you're a sexist who is allowing an unjust status quo reign due to your passive acceptance. Either way, I was the asshole. Good news was, I was used to being the asshole.

I headed inside and found a board with office and room assignments. It didn't take long to find *Dr. E. Travis, 308.* I hit the stairs and headed up, but not before seeing the pressed crowd at the front entrance and silently thanked Andie for the advice about the back door. I knew I'd have to phrase that different when I told the story to Gretchen later. I knew I'd never use the phrase "advice about the back door" around Jammer.

A guy in his late 30s in a gray Armani suit, believe it or not, doesn't really stand out in a college campus. Students think you're a professor. Professors think you're there to talk to one of their colleagues, or are some flunky with the administration. The most out of place thing about me was the fact that I refused to put a corporate noose around my neck, so I could leave my top shirt button undone, and the fact I was wearing my black and white Chucks.

I got to the third floor and saw that even office numbers were along the front of the building and odd office numbers were along the back. I headed down until I came to office 308. The door was closed; it was outside his posted office hours. I did see he had posted a note stating that Dr. Travis wasn't going to be holding office hours or class on Friday due to a personal commitment that day.

Friday was the day the Spear of Destiny auction was supposed to be going down.

Out of my peripheral vision, I saw someone come up toward me as I studied the note on the door. I looked and saw a nineteen or twenty year old mousy-haired brunette girl with her hair done up in a side ponytail. She seemed nice enough but her glasses were so thick they could have stopped a 9mm bullet fired point blank.

"You look a little old for a student." The retainer in her mouth slurred her S's a bit so it sounded like she said *shdudent*.

I waved my hand in front of her face. "These aren't the droids you're looking for. Move along."

I turned and headed back down the hallway toward the stairs, leaving the girl stunned in my wake. I was actually pleased with myself that I threw a *Star Wars* reference at her instead of simply telling her to fuck off. Maybe I was maturing; maybe I was becoming a better person. Maybe I just liked Sir Alec Guinness, who knew what the truth was? Maybe it was relative?

I went back down the stairs two at a time until I went out the back door and started jogging toward the nearest parking lot. I managed to catch up with Andie. "Hey." I slowed to a walk as I fell in next to her. "Mind giving me a ride?"

She laughed. "Sure, you finished with your secret mission?"

"Eh, more recon than secret mission, but yeah." I took a couple of deep breaths trying to slow my heart rate back after the jog. Mind if I ask you something?"

"Sure." She looked over to me curiously.

"So, I see someone checking you out, objectifying you and all. Am I a misogynist if I say something because I'm assuming you can't take care of your own shit. Or am I a sexist if I don't say anything because I'm letting demeaning shit go on?" I glanced to her and there was confusion in her brown eyes. "I mean, how do I walk out of that situation and not be an asshole?"

"You are an asshole, Nick." She laughed and nudged my arm. "But a likable one."

"Thanks. But seriously."

We got out to the parking lot and moved to her green Nissan Jetta. She unlocked the doors with a fob. "You don't win. It's a Catch-22." She opened the driver's side door and looked over the top of the car to me apologetically. "Sorry, Nick, sometimes you're just fucked either way."

Before I opened the door I took out my flask and took a slug of the Macallan, with it I took a metaphorical dose of Fuck-It-All as I slid the flask back in my pocket.

Chapter Eleven: Surveillance Can Be A Pleasant Date

Happy Together by The Turtles

It was dark by the time Gretchen got off shift, but not so late that we seemed shifty sitting at a cafe across from Wedge Wood Towers Luxury Condo Apartments. Gretchen had on her black yoga pants, pouch belt, combat boots, and a plain gray T-shirt under her leather jacket. We sat at a table outside and lazily watched the front entrance of the Wedge Wood.

The waitress taking care of our section walked over and adjusted the temp on one of the outdoor heaters as the fall chill was settling around everyone. "That's better." She smiled and smoothed her pink and brown smock before taking out her pad and pen. "Okay, welcome to Bennet Sister's Scones." She smiled so big and was so perky she had to be on antidepressants. Anyone who acted that happy had to be into some dark shit when they were home alone. "What can I get you?"

Gretchen smiled sweetly as she studied the menu and looked up from the laminated card. "May I have the Ebony and Ivory scones and a chicory coffee?"

The waitress smiled. "Oh, that is my absolute favorite."

"The scones or the coffee?" Gretchen asked politely.

"The scones." The waitress bounced as she said it.

Gretchen smile brightened. "Oh good, I was hoping they'd be as good as they sound."

"You will not be let down." The waitress smiled as she scribbled the order on the pad. "And you, sir?"

"Scone and hot chocolate," I told her as I barely took my eyes off the apartment building to glance up to her.

"What kind?" She was chipper enough to have animated birds fly through her windows in the morning to help her dress.

"Plain." I watched a couple enter the apartment building and wave to the guy working the front desk.

"We have assorted sweet and savory scones." She leaned in to push the menu toward my hand.

I looked up to her curiously. "Do you have plain ones?"

She nodded with eyes bright as a 500 lumen Tac Lights.

"Then," I said slowly, "you can tell Lizzy, Jane, and Minnie and Fanny that I'll take a plain one."

"Who are they?" she asked curiously about the unfamiliar names.

I thought about telling her but decided it was just simpler to just reiterate, "Just plain ones and a hot chocolate."

"Okay," she said ruefully as she wrote it down with the hesitation of a loved one who just wasn't able to talk the person they care about the most in the world out of Double or Nothing Russian Roulette. She took the laminated menu card and headed back inside to put in our order.

"Did you just drop an Austen reference?" Gretchen asked playfully.

I gestured to the sign. "It says fucking Bennet Sisters... I can't be the first goddamn person to ever put that together."

Gretchen laughed but nodded in agreement. We sat on the same side of the table and I slipped my arm around her shoulder and she leaned her head against my shoulder.

"Hey," I said awkwardly.

"Everything groovy?" she asked as she glanced around in case I'd seen something and she'd missed the threat.

"I'm pretty sure I love you." I just put it out there. Some people play games, and some people can actually make things sound good when they speak. *Has a way with words* has never been a description attributable to me.

She snort-laughed and nestled her head back into the crook of my neck and shoulder. "I kinda figured that out when you came to rescue me." She reached her arm under mine and around my back. "If it makes you feel better, I can tell you exactly when I realized I loved you."

"Oh, yeah?"

She chuckled and kissed my cheek. "The difference between can and may."

I laughed. Out of the corner of my eye, I saw a white panel van sitting at the corner. A guy in slacks and a Members Only windbreaker moved to the van and hopped inside. As soon as the side door was closed the van started moving with a squeal of tires.

The waitress brought Gretchen her coffee and me a hot chocolate with so much cream I couldn't see the liquid underneath. I sprinkled a little cinnamon on it and started stirring.

"I'm surprised you don't drink coffee," Gretchen commented as she sat up and took a sip.

"Coffee tastes like the water that drips off a whore's perineum when she showers after a long and grueling day of work." I took a sip of the hot chocolate from the spoon before setting it on the saucer.

Gretchen sipped her black chicory coffee. "Mmmm, hot whore taint water."

I laughed and was grateful I wasn't swallowing because had I been it would have come out of my nose. I picked up my hot mug and sipped as I watched another person enter the apartment high-rise.

"They are using some kind of scan card to get through the door," Gretchen commented.

"Yeah, they hold it up to the touch plate. I'm guessing the guy at the desk could buzz us in but I'm betting he'd have to call someone for confirmation and we'd have to sign in."

Gretchen nodded in agreement. "Could you boost a card?"

"Yeah," I said slowly. "But the question is how long till they notice it? And if I get pinched doing it that's the game."

She again nodded in agreement. "Do you think he has it in there?"

"I dunno what to think at the moment." I took a longer sip as I watched the front entrance.

"Liar." She smiled.

"Huh?"

"You have a plan, you just don't want to tell me because you don't like it." She looked up to me with raised eyebrows.

I bit my lip and looked back to the door. "Well, yeah."

"What is it?" she asked as she reached up with her finger to turn my chin so our eyes met.

"I think he's going to try and boost every bit of cash brought to his auction for the Spear, then walk off with all of it. The cash, the Spear, the lot."

She nodded. "Okay." I've never heard an "okay" sound so much like an "and."

"Half of me wants to let him do it, then we roll him up and take all of it." It didn't sound crazy until you started thinking of all the unknowns. Some concepts are great, but the practicality is fucked; fuck you, communism.

We looked back to the doors as the waitress brought out our plates of scones.

"I've been trying to think of potential buyers," she said around a mouthful of scone.

"Any ideas?" I watched the deskman, who was an at least apparently unarmed security guard, get up and go to the bathroom. I started a timer on my phone.

"Well, I think the obvious buyer is going to be Cardinal Hines." She emptied her mug of coffee.

Cardinal Hines was a connected son of a bitch. Cardinal in the Catholic Church, he'd been asked about the possibility of being the first American Pope but he'd flat out said he would never want that; because as much as the world was his community, he felt he could better serve the Lord by serving at the level he was at and never wanted more. His little brother was a congressman. Their dad had made his money in some industry or another, but ironically none of it had been condiments. Cardinal Hines had had money in the housing market before the big crash but sold right before the market decided to shit the bed. If God had told him to sell, he'd not shared the message.

Gretchen was right; he had money to blow on it, and it wasn't unbelievable that a cardinal in the Catholic Church would want a little trinket that had popped the side of Christ.

"Do you have an angle to work?" I asked her as I bit into the scone. Scones had always struck me as just someone's fucked up attempt at a muffin or someone's pretentious attempt at a biscuit. They just seemed unnecessary, but this one was good.

"Not yet." There was a bit of defeat in her voice as she confessed it.

"Strong arm him into making him take one of us to the auction?" I suggested.

"It's a thought, but I'm not sure how good of one it is," she agreed.

"I think the best play is trying to get it before the auction happens." I stopped the timer as the guard came back to his desk: five minutes, four seconds. "There's less heat that way."

She nodded in agreement.

We finished our scones and Gretchen paid the check with crumpled one-dollar bills that I wondered where they had been stuffed earlier in the day but knew better to ask. Honestly, as much as I wondered, I didn't care.

Through the windows I saw the doors, the front desk, then there was a bank of elevators; on the other side of the elevators was the set of doors heading out into the parking deck.

"That might be something," I muttered.

"Access through the parking deck?" Gretchen asked curiously.

I nodded. "It's a thought. We wouldn't have to make our way past the security guy going that route."

"The security guy isn't armed," she pointed out. "Sure you don't want to shoot the security cameras through the door and go in with your .45 in his face?" She smiled over to me devilishly.

My eyes met hers. "You're never going to let me live that down are you?"

"I dunno." She leaned her head back onto my shoulder. "It's not every day you get to see your boyfriend rob a convenient store is it?"

"Me robbed?" I said in mock shock. "Don't you mean WE robbed?"

"Hush you." She goosed me in the ribs.

We stood and walked arm in arm around the block watching the building getting a view of all the sides. It was along the back that I saw a potential way in. The second-floor balconies weren't that high up. We headed down the alley and Gretchen kept watch as I tried. I let myself get angry. I thought about the fact that there wasn't a biopic of the World War Two-through-X1 years of Chuck Yeager's life and I felt the rage in the back of my head. I jumped and managed to clear the distance to grab the rail of one of the second-floor balconies.

I hung for a second and then let myself swing to give me some momentum. I let go and kept my feet and knees together, knees slightly bent. I hit on the balls of my feet and rolled onto my hip, my thigh and then onto my back before rolling up on my feet. It wasn't a perfect Parachute Landing Fall, but I'd definitely had worse PLFs back in the Army.

"You're going to ruin your suit doing stuff like that," Gretchen chided, but her smile belayed any seriousness in her tone. She patted the back of my jacket then patted the back of my pants before giving my ass a squeeze. I jumped a bit and she laughed. We made our way back around and to the front of the building. As we passed the windows by the security desk, I managed to snap a picture of the bulletin board.

As soon as we were clear we started zooming in on the notices on the board. The third one we zoomed in on turned out to be the jackpot. I reread it to make sure I hadn't misread it. I hadn't, I can be accurate in my initial assessments.

"So," I smirked down at Gretchen, getting a slight peek into the neck of her T-shirt, "Dr. Travis is having a wine tasting party tomorrow night for everyone in the building."

"And guests are invited," Gretchen finished with that mischievous grin of hers that must have been the bane of her parents and I could never get enough of. "Too bad you're a Scotch guy and don't know anything about wine other than Pino Noir goes with steak."

"What more is there to know?"

She rolled her eyes.

"Don't worry, I got a guy for wine." I pulled out my phone and she watched curiously as I held the phone to my ear as it rang. "Hey, Switch, want to go to a wine party tomorrow?"

Chapter Twelve: An Emergency and a Clean-Up

Thunderstruck by AC/DC

T he only reason I answered the call was because Gretchen asked me why I was dodging the call. I gave her my logical and well-reasoned answer, and she gave me an admonishing look that shamed me into hitting the green icon as opposed to the red one or finish listening to my Breaking Benjamin ring tone. With my parentage and family tree, I understood it was strange to think it, but thank God for Gretchen.

The front door had been attacked with a hooligan tool and a sledgehammer. It was barely hanging on askew on the top hinge; the bottom two had torn themselves free. I had my pistol in my grip as I went through the door and cleared left before sweeping right. Gretchen drew an ASP collapsible club out of each sleeve of her jacket and snapped them to their full length. We saw the door into the hallway torn free. I took point; Gretchen followed close behind.

I looked into the room beyond the Faraday hallway and saw the guy with a hooligan tool smashing monitors. I felt the anger. I didn't even have to focus. I snapped off a shot and it slammed into the back of the man's head and splattered his face over the smashed monitor and desk in front of him. I flowed through the door and button-hooked left to clear before sweeping back across the room.

The guy with the sledgehammer had been in the right corner. He might have gotten me in the back had Gretchen not been there. He was moving toward me raising the hammer. Gretchen got between us as I was sweeping back around. Her left ASP caught the guy in the left elbow. The guy's arm turned to jelly and the hammer fell out of his left hand. He clung to it with the right but was off balance. Gretchen then almost simultaneously caught the guy's right knee causing it to buckle. The guy dropped the hammer as his head hit the wall on his gravity-fueled voyage to the floor.

The guy was out of the fight but he wasn't out. She held the ASPs together and plopped on the man's chest, her knees over his shoulders helping pin them as she leaned the clubs over his throat until he turned red, then purple. His body shook before he went limp. She leaned in.

"I'm pretty sure he's dead," I told her after a bit.

"How are you sure?" She let up on the clubs and checked for a pulse.

"He shit himself," I said dryly as the I could see the man's khakis were dark with piss, and the smell of shit filled my nostrils. Gretchen climbed off the corpse and I made a quick sweep of the rest of the place.

"Nick!" Gretchen called from the control room. "We got company!" I ran back as fast as my Chucks would carry me. I looked to one of the surviving monitors and saw two white vans and eight guys in Tac Gear climbing out. "They're Teutonic Knights," she lamented.

"You okay?" I asked. It couldn't be easy being forced to go up against people who had been allies, friends, and compatriots. I knew

I would be fucked if I were ever thrown up against my old Airborne Infantry Company. It was just a reminder of what she'd done for me. What she'd given up for me, even before she'd known she was my soulmate.

She bit her lip hard but she nodded.

"You don't have to do this," I told her. I felt my fingers milk the grip of my 1911. I felt the itch in the back of my mind; the call to action, the lure of the Fiery Sword. I felt the Wrath wanting to lash out and burn the eight men out front.

I also knew I had to go. If they flash-banged us inside we were done. I started running down the hallway. I had been good in a gunfight before. Now, because of the Fiery Sword, the Wrath of God, I was preternatural.

I saw the barrel of a shotgun barely poking past the edge of the door. That was a mistake. Back in the Army, we'd referred to it as "flagging" the barrel. You'd never want to do that for the reasoning the man holding the shotgun quickly found out, but never really got to profit from the experience. I grabbed the barrel just above the end and yanked hard away and down. It dragged the man holding it off balance and he stumbled in front of the doorway. I pushed the 1911 to his ear and sprayed his brain matter away from me. The shot caused burns around the guy's ear, but he'd never notice.

I stepped into the doorway and my shoulder nudged the amazingly fresh corpse out of the way as it fell to the ground. I shot the Number Two man in the stack right in the middle of his face. The bullet punched into the bridge of his nose and spilled blood and brain into the back of his black Kevlar helmet.

At this point, the hit teams knew something was seriously wrong with their plan, which must have looked amazing when it was on paper.

I stepped back into the door and used it for cover as I aimed at the van. I saw the first man coming around the front to take aim at me in the doorway. I did everything proper: proper sight picture, proper sight alignment, proper stance, proper grip, proper trigger press, and the hammer of my 1911 fell, striking the firing pin and punching the primer. The bullet flew out of the end of the five-inch barrel at close to eight-hundred-and-thirty feet per second. The last thing the guy must have seen was the flash from my barrel before the round punched through his Wiley X goggles and into his eye, punching out the back of the ocular bone and scrambling the brain matter behind it like eggs for an omelet.

I could see a man behind the van through the passenger and driver's side windows. Most of his body was under cover of the doors, but his shoulders and head were exposed. I shifted my aim and fired my fifth shot for the day, and fourth in about a second and a half. The bullet pierced through windows and found purchase in the man's unarmored neck just behind where the jaw met the ear. He fell out of sight.

I had two more rounds in the magazine and one in the chamber. I'd love to have tac-reloaded but had the feeling that there wasn't time.

I rolled to the right back into the door and dropped to my knee. I saw as the third man in the stack by the door charged forward past and over the corpses of his friends. His submachine gun was aimed from his shoulder and he swept the barrel past me over my head. He had forgotten that combat is a multi-dimensional affair. I was right at the level of his crotch so that's where my bullet found a home. It hammered his pelvis and shattered his hip. From the gush of blood, it didn't take a doctor to know that there was an arterial wound even as the guy was falling.

I rolled to my left coming up on my knee just in time to see the surprised look of the Number Four man as he started to enter the doorway. My gun was aimed up so my round caught him under the jaw snapping his head back as the bullet passed through his mouth and out the back of his head.

I rolled again out of the funnel of the door and had my back against the wall as I started dropping my magazine. I was starting to get dizzy from all the rolling. There was nothing left in the magazine but there still was one round left in the chamber. I was pulling a fresh mag from my shoulder rig when I saw the man shot through the hip reaching for his sidearm. He was dead, but he didn't know it yet, but that didn't mean he couldn't kill me either.

That last round in the chamber put him out of his misery. The way he was screaming you knew it had to be miserable. Shattered bone grating on shattered bone as he bled out. But even with that, he was still trying to gun up and draw down on me. You had to respect that. That didn't stop me from giving him my last .45ACP round.

I got the magazine rammed home in the grip of the 1911 and dropped the slide. I stuffed the pistol in the front of my pants; the barrel was warm after eight rounds but not unbearably so yet. I reached over and unclipped the sling from an old M-16 A1 that the Tac Team member had been carrying. It had a modern Magpul polymer magazine, but the rest of the weapon screamed Desert Storm. The trigger was a custom job though. He hadn't carried it because it was the hottest new thing on the block, but because it was his gun love, cared for and tended with loving care.

I used the man's corpse as cover as I lay prone and got the gun to my shoulder. Gunfire was coming from the van peppering the door, a shotgun and an MP-5 blasting 9mm rounds at automatic. But their fire was coming in at chest level, passing over my head.

I fired two rounds quick, and it was easy with that modified trigger having almost competition weight to it instead of being mil-spec. The previous owner had a good zero on the sights. At twenty yards headshots were simple if you knew what you were doing, and the man with the MP-5 dearly paid for it.

I shifted aim and saw the man with the shotgun turn to run. He didn't get far. He didn't have side plates in his plate carrier and the four rounds I punched into his side didn't kill him, but he wasn't going to live much longer after he hit the dirt with no ceremony.

I slowly stood and dusted myself off. I put my 1911 back in the shoulder holster. I knew it wasn't sporting, but I walked from man to man and pushed the barrel of the M-16 to their head and snapped off a round. They were already dead, but an ounce of prevention is worth a pound of cure, I reckoned.

Finally when I came back around the van and saw Gretchen already throwing weapons and Tac Gear in one of the vans. I grabbed the legs of one of the dead men and started dragging him to the other van. I stopped about halfway and stripped the body of his weapons and gear. He didn't have any ID. I threw the weapons and gear in the van Gretchen was loading and went to the next body to do the same. There was Tac Gear, weapons, and ammo, but there were no IDs. Who knew what their plan would have been if they'd been stopped by the cops?

"Thanks," she told me.

"For what?" I asked as I shut the van door.

Her large, liquid large eyes met mine. "For making sure I didn't have to."

I pulled her into my arms and kissed her forehead. "I'm sorry it has to be this way."

She wrapped her arms around my waist and squeezed. "You are worth it. Even when you sing in the shower."

I chuckled, before offering soberly, "If you ever need to talk about it, I'm good for it."

"I know. But not right now, okay?" She looked up at me expectantly.

I nodded. She let go and we got to work pulling the bodies into the second fan. Moving a dead body, as I learned in the Army, is a pain in the ass. They leak, they feel off, and they are completely uncooperative or appreciative of all the damned work you're putting into things. It took us twenty minutes to put the ten stripped-down corpses in the second van.

Gretchen pointed to the first two we had killed. "These guys were decoys to draw us out. The Tac Teams were here for the kill."

I nodded. "Yeah, they weren't packing any beanbag rounds this time."

"So the question is"—Gretchen paused—"were they here for me, you or both?"

"Doesn't matter," I reassured her. "They got and will continue to fucking get both."

She smiled, but I could tell it was forced. No one should have to have their team turn on them, nor turn on their team. It was just a reminder of what all I owed Gretchen.

We locked up the body van. When it came time to leave I'd drive it somewhere, diligently obeying traffic laws on the way, and then torch it. We looked around outside, and even though there were blood stains on concrete all the obvious signs of the butchery had been removed, or at least hidden until I drove away in the Charnel Mobile.

Even though we were sure the place was clear we swept it again anyway. Gretchen had one of the shotguns in her hands making her slightly more combat effective than she had been with the ASPs.

When we were sure it was clear I looked to a video camera up in the corner of the room.

"Okay, you can come out now." I beckoned with the barrel of my 1911.

Slowly a wall panel opened revealing a panic room inside. It was well stocked and apportioned with food, snacks, and sundries. There was a bed and a bank of monitors.

Out of here emerged the pajama-clad form of Megan Tara Meyer. When I say pajama what I mean is wearing a Chinese knockoff Kimono. Strands of strawberry blonde hair stuck out from under her geisha wig. Yet apparently she either slept with the geisha makeup on, or she had fixed it inside the panic room while Gretchen and I had cleared house. She had a satchel over her shoulder that had a laptop and God knows what else.

She looked at me with blood on my hands and a 1911 in my grip. She looked at Gretchen with blood on her hands and a 12-gauge pump shotgun in her hands and a smile on her face.

"Gretchen," I gestured to Gretchen, "this is Megan Tara Meyer, or as she's going to try to get you to call her The Grand Vizier Megatron Terabyte the Cyber Samurai."

Gretchen smiled and slung the shotgun. She wiped her hands on a rag and applied some hand sanitizer before walking over to the confused Tara and wrapped the taller woman up in a large, warm, and from my point of view, very disheartening hug. Gretchen looked up into the confused made-up face. "I'm Gretchen, and I just love you. We are going to be the best of friends!"

...Fuck my life.

Chapter Thirteen: Carl Paxton's Steak House

The Way You Look Tonight by Frank Sinatra

I've never been one to claim that I have had epiphanies after combat, or fighting, or anything like that. But that doesn't mean I was so dense to see Gretchen needed to talk, needed a break. Tara gave us a big explanation about the Akashic record that boiled down to "when you look into the Akashic Record it looks back at you." So from her searches for us into the Spear of Destiny, they'd been able to find her. Gretchen was convinced that it was her old crew, The Teutonic Knights. Not the public charitable organization that you could find on the internet and the news, but serious old-school Crusader pipe-hitting motherfuckers.

The power of the Sword made me better than I had been before when it came to fighting. Used to be I would have had to concentrate like an idiot at a spelling bee to pull off headshots like

I'd done earlier. Now, I just had to think it, and it basically happened. I'd always been able to drive tacks with a rifle, but pistols kicked my ass at this range. Not anymore though.

We took the vans. Gretchen drove the not-shot-up van with the weapons and other gear with the distraught Megatron as her passenger. I took the shot-up one with corpses. Much to my dismay, Gretchen had taken to the Cyber Samurai the way I took to the eighteen-year-old single malt Macallan.

Tara had grabbed a few things but for the most part abandoned the building she'd been living and working in. Apparently, her money was funneled through so many shells and banks and whatnot that if it were traced back far enough whoever was looking would find it belonged to Mrs. Ethel Babette Troffaunt of some shit suburb of New Orleans, who also had happened to have died ten years before. The warehouse office we'd just left wasn't even in the name of Megan Tara Meyer.

I drove the van with the shot-out driver's and passenger side windows stacked with corpses in the back hoping like hell I didn't get pulled over. Luckily I didn't, or things would have gotten a whole lot worse. We ditched the van of corpses down by the docks. Instead of just ditching it I decided to light it on fire. I used gas and a lighter instead of the Fiery Sword, but I could still feel the pull of the Sword. I could feel the lust of the Father to burn and destroy. For a while, I thought the Dali Lama could probably deal with this better than me because there were times it felt good.

I climbed in the van and Gretchen drove to a storage place she and I had paid cash a few days ago for "just in case," and stashed the guns and kit. Then I hopped behind the wheel and drove us to where Switch had parked the RV and was working on his potential mayhem. The Grand Vizier was hesitant but she eventually agreed to go into Switch's care. Switch was, justified in my opinion, in his reluctance to take her.

After that, I drove us to the mall. I hate malls. I hate crowds of people. I hate browsing instead of shopping. I hated everything but the Cinnabon there. We wandered shops, much to Gretchen's confusion until we found her a black dress with a silvery belt. She tried it on at my request and when I saw her in it I took the tag and paid for it. Agnes might get onto me about the money but I didn't care. Next, we managed to find her shoes to go with it. That took longer than it should have, but we were shopping for shoes for a woman, so it was expected.

She looked like she should have been on the arm of some douchebag Ivy League CEO as the second wife or first trophy wife. I wish I could have gotten her some jewelry but I wouldn't have known what to get and I couldn't have afforded to get her what she deserved, especially considering I couldn't really afford the dress or shoes I'd already gotten her or the dinner we were about to go to.

Carl Paxton had been a high school football star and then had gone on to a great college career and been in the contention for the Heisman. He spent four seasons in the NFL as an offensive lineman. In that time, he'd bought four car dealerships and a restaurant, Paxton's Steakhouse. The genius of Carl wasn't in his business acumen but in his ability to find competent people then get out of their way. Paxton's Steakhouse didn't have a chef; it had two. Louise was a classically trained French chef, and Toby Lowery was raised in a chuck wagon slinging meat for ranch hands. Toby ended up winning a couple of grilling and smoking championships.

Louise and Toby had met when Carl put them together; they'd instantly hated each other. Louise thought Toby was a lowbrow cretin armed with tongs and a fork. Toby thought Louise was an uppity bitch with her nose in the clouds so she could look down at him even though he was taller.

A year later Carl Paxton paid for their wedding reception.

A few years ago someone had tried to shake down Carl with a scam about business permits. They said his paperwork was jacked up and started putting him through the red tape ringer. Carl's lawyer started fighting the good fight but it was going to take time. Carl hired me and got out of my way. It took two weeks but at the end of it everything was squared up and the permit asshole was arrested for extortion or some other douchebag crime. Now Carl was too much of a businessman to give me free food, but he did promise me a table any time I wanted one.

We walked in and were greeted by Carl himself. He liked to hang out at the restaurant and be seen. I think it reminded him he was still someone even though his three-hundred-pound frame was no longer pure muscle. I'm pretty sure he could have palmed my head and crushed it, and he nearly knocked me over when he slapped me on the back.

"Decker," his deep voice boomed with the same distinction as his ebony skin clashed with his white suit. "My man, I didn't know you could afford to eat here."

"Normally, no, but I have a date." I gestured to Gretchen.

Carl was a foot and a half taller than Gretchen and his hand swallowed hers even as he bent down to kiss her hand. *"Achante, Mademoiselle.* If you find anything here to not be to your satisfaction you come to Carl and Carl will take care of you." She smiled and he stood back to his full gigantic height, "Now, I just have to ask, why is an angel as lovely as you with Mr. Decker?" He looked at me apologetically. "Sorry, Nick, you're my boy and all, but this angel is out of your league." He gestured up and down Gretchen's dusky petite form as if I'd never checked it out on my own and he was revealing something new to me.

Carl took Gretchen's arm and took us to a table without waiting for my answer.

"I didn't catch your name." Carl smiled as he led her through the restaurant.

"Gretchen." Her smile was infectious.

Carl would have made an amazing damned politician but he'd decided he preferred honest money as opposed to, you know, being a politician. He held the seat out for Gretchen and she sat demurely as he gently edged the chair under her even though, had he wanted, he could have lifted her and the chair one-handed. He laid her napkin across her lap. I had to do all this for myself, but I wasn't going to complain.

Carl snapped his fingers and a short, but well-proportioned dark-skinned man with a shaved head that shined in the low lights of the restaurant dining room appeared. He wore a white jacket with black slacks. His bow tie was the most perfect knot I've ever seen.

"This," Carl introduced us, but really just speaking to Gretchen, "is Sinclair. He waits on me when I dine here and he is going to take care of you. Sinclair, this is Nick Decker and the lovely Gretchen." Carl laughed at his own impending wit. "Don't get them mixed up!"

Sinclair smiled too broadly, to be honest. He was playing a part, pandering to his boss. But in a lot of ways that was probably what made him seem to be a great employee.

Sinclair gave us menus and filled our crystal goblets with water then stepped away to give us a moment.

Gretchen leaned in and whispered, "Nick, what are we doing here? It a job?"

I smirked and quietly chuckled. But I felt the blood rushing to my face and I knew she could probably feel the embarrassment glow off me like an awkward light bulb. "We've, uh, never had a, you know, a real date."

It took a moment for that to sink in but finally, her smile bloomed on her lips. I could tell some of the other patrons were put off and stared at the ink across her shoulders and down her arms, readily visible in the spaghetti-strapped dress but I didn't care. The world could melt way and I'd have been okay with Gretchen.

She smiled and looked down at the menu. "Well, if you expect me to put out you better spring for lobster."

I laughed and sat my menu down.

"You not even going to look at it?" she asked curiously.

I gave her a crooked grin. "Nope."

"You eat here so often you know what you want?" She arched her eyebrow over the top of the menu.

"I've eaten here once, and just know what I want."

Sinclair walked over with two wine glasses and an opened bottle of Pinot Noir. He poured a sample in each. I stuck my nose in the glass and inhaled because that's what I thought you were supposed to do then downed the sample. I looked to Gretchen and we both nodded. Sinclair poured from the bottle with a twist of his wrist at the end of each. After filling both he set the bottle down then shook my hand, palming me a note like we were spies in a Cold War story. I held the note under the edge of the table and read, "Customer paid the uncorking but didn't want the bottle, *gratis*."

I slid the note in my pocket and glanced around till I saw Carl. He grinned like the Cheshire cat who had just gotten away with murder. I nodded my thanks.

Sinclair didn't bring a pad, pen or paper when he came to take our order. His accent seemed Jamaican but honestly could have been any of the islands of even West African and I couldn't have been able to tell the difference, but I would have put money on Jamaican. Gretchen ordered a petite filet, au gratin potatoes, and truffle mac and cheese. I ordered a large filet and house fries. I was the type of guy that Toby Lowery loved and Louise despised. Gretchen accepted the house salad and I politely informed Sinclair, "I don't eat the food that food eats." He gave the same patronizing smile to me he gave Carl. I didn't buy the look but accepted he was good.

He brought out bread, which turned out to be homemade mini baguettes that were about six inches long. It came with two different kinds of butter, one whipped, the other whipped with cinnamon. It arrived with Gretchen's salad drizzled with a homemade vinaigrette. Gretchen didn't want the heel pieces of bread and I liked them. So that worked out.

I smeared some of the cinnamon butter on the heel slice, more than a cardiologist would have preferred.

She dug her fork into her salad and smiled. "So..."

I chuckled. "Well, you said there were files on me. I think I know everything important about you. But how about some details?"

She looked at me cautiously. "You sure you want to know?"

I laughed so hard wine almost came out of my nose. "Gretchen, I drink too much, I'm basically broke and I'm the Devil's goddamned nephew. You know all that." I reached over and took her non-fork hand in mine. "You know all that and you're still with me for some insane fucking reason." I squeezed her hand and my shit-brown eyes met the dark ethereal pools of beauty that God gave her to see out of. "You really think there is anything you can tell me that's going to scare me the fuck off?"

Chapter Fourteen: The Making of Gretchen Told Over Steak

God Love Her by Toby Keith

"What's the female form of bastard?" she asked inquisitively.

I shrugged and leaned back in my seat. "I dunno."

She sighed. "Well, whatever it is, that's me."

"So your folks weren't married?" I asked and sipped the wine. I didn't want to pull out my flask in a place as fancy as this. I wanted a drink, but I still wanted some of the bottle there when the food arrived. Sometimes life is walking on the edge of a razor.

"As far as I was told they only met once." She smiled wistfully; it was a good look on her. "But the night was defined as magical apparently."

"Well, it's better than the alternative I guess."

She looked at me curiously. "What's the alternative?"

I crossed my arms and thought. "Product of a magical night seems better than the outcome of a pity fuck right?"

She laughed. I'd never feel like a sap admitting I loved her laugh. "Yeah, I don't think I was the product of mom tossing a favor to the old man."

I chuckled. "Well, that's something. Was it love?"

She grimaced a bit. "I don't know. I'd like to think so, but who knows?" She looked down and pushed her fork into her salad with a soft crunch sound as the tines tore through lettuce and into a crouton soaking in the vinaigrette pooled in the bottom of the bowl. "Mom grew up in one of the Order's convents like I did."

"What about your dad?" I set my elbows on the table then remembered you are not supposed to do that so I pulled them back and crossed my forearms in front of me to try and cover my *faux pas*.

"He was a Chaplain in the Navy." She smiled wistfully. "He'd been a Marine scout sniper in Vietnam. Apparently, while he was humping the bush in 'Nam he finished a mission and found God. When he got his discharge he went to seminary and became a Baptist minister. Then he went to a recruiting station and fought paperwork and bureaucracy to become a Navy Chaplain. He spent a few trips on ships but hated it. He bribed and bartered and battered his way through orders to get assigned to a Marine Infantry unit."

She paused and I smiled. "Once a Grunt, huh?"

She chuckled and ate a forkful of salad. She kept her eyes locked to mine till she took down a sip of wine. "Always a Grunt, I guess." Her smile was soft, her eyes glazed with memory. "He served in Grenada, Panama, Desert Storm. But everything ends eventually."

"The up or out?" I asked.

She nodded. "He got promoted to the point he wasn't out with the guys anymore. I don't think dad wanted to be a preacher or an administrator, which is what I guess everyone in the military is once you hit a certain level. He wanted to be a chaplain." She chuckled sadly. "A war priest, I guess. Maybe dad's God wasn't purely the Christian God but the Warrior God. The one who was with David when he stepped up to Goliath, the one who tore down the walls of Jericho."

I sipped my wine. "Blessed be the Lord, my rock who trains my hands for war and fingers to fight."

"*Psalms 144, verse 1.*" She smiled, but it still felt melancholy. "Mom found him, despondent and drinking like the sergeant he'd been in 'Nam. Trying to find the meaning in the bottom of a bottle he used to find in the job. I guess, as much as dad had found God he needed war. The time came, the Navy let him go. He tried preaching but it wasn't the same."

I could get that. I've never been the best with people, but it was tough connecting with people who lived lives with hyperbolic hyperbole. I knew where I stood with Jammer because we'd earned that. I didn't understand how someone who had never been in the shit could say "I'd do anything for my friends." It was hard to connect to people you didn't have a gauge on.

"Dad wasn't a preacher for people, he was a chaplain for Marines. Does that make sense?" There was a pleading tone to Gretchen's voice. Like she needed me to understand. As if she believed my understanding would somehow make what I knew was coming understandable.

I nodded.

"He killed himself three months before I was born." She reached up and wiped the corner of her eyes with her thumb. She was doing an amazing job of keeping a brave face; the quiver of her lip gave it away. I wasn't going to call her on it. "Not that he knew I was coming."

I reached across the table and grabbed her hand. I felt her thumb brush along one of my knuckles and I felt the dampness of her thumb tip glisten on my skin.

"Mom thought it was important that I know I came from 'Pious Warrior Stock' as she called it."

"What about her?" I asked, trying to subtly change the subject for Gretchen's sake.

"She'd come up in the Order. She said there were two great sacrifices that had to be paid for the greater good. Sacrificing oneself and sacrificing one's daughter." Gretchen didn't seem disturbed by the implications of what she was saying.

"What about if you'd been a guy?"

She laughed and made a playful kissy face. "Then you'd be gay probably."

I laughed.

"Coming up was"—she chewed her lip looking for the right adjective before settling on—"eclectic."

I didn't ask anything, but apparently, the way I raised my eyebrow was enough to warrant further explanation.

"I grew up studying gymnastics. I spent a few years studying dance. I spent a few years at Iga-ryu studying reiki and other stuff." Her speech slowed as she said "other stuff."

"What other stuff?" I pressed.

"Ninja stuff." She shrugged with a disconcerting nonchalance as if *ninja stuff* was the same as saying *I bought eggs at the store because I was out*. She smiled. "I got my ink in Japan."

"Oh, yeah?"

She chuckled. "My first actual mission for the Order was there. I worked out finding proof a Yakuza boss was scheming with a Triad to put another Yakuza member out of business. The Yakuza guy wanted his rival's territory, and the Triad wanted to be the sole provider of weaponry to the organization. I was told to clean it up."

I arched my eyebrows. "And did you?"

She sipped her wine and nodded. "I let the Yakuza guy know what was going on and he cleaned both sides of the house so to speak. It was bloody, but neat and tidy nonetheless."

"What's that got to do with your ink?"

"Well, the Yakuza guy rewarded me with the services his own personal tattoo artist. So I got the Cross to represent the Order and the wings for me." She twisted her arm to get a glance at her wings.

"What's the order like?" I asked curiously.

She thought about it for a moment. "Purposeful." We let go of each other's hand as Sinclair came out with another waiter carrying our food. The plates with our steaks were set before us. The sides were arranged in the no man's land between the entrees. Sinclair topped off our wine with his expert twisting pour.

"What was the Army like?" she asked as she started cutting her steak.

"I loved it deployed." I cut a piece that was a touch too large to be polite. "I hated it in the rear." I crammed the steak in my mouth and bit down.

"That's what she said." She smiled demurely. "Lots of people hate it in the rear."

That got a laugh out of me even as I was chewing.

"What do you mean?" she asked as I nearly choked.

After I finally managed to swallow I started cutting a new piece. "I loved being deployed. I mean, I joined the Army to break things, blow shit up, and shoot motherfuckers who had it coming in the face. So busting doors in Iraq and patrolling the Afghani-Paki border, it's all I wanted."

"And in the position of sodomy?" she asked with a raised eyebrow.

"Huh?" I asked with obvious confusion.

Her smile was completely juxtaposed ladylike. "In the rear."

I laughed again.

"I fuckin' hated it. I mean, the shit that didn't matter started mattering more than the shit that should." I didn't know if that made sense or not to anyone but me.

"What do you mean?"

"I was an Infantry guy. So if it didn't make me a better killer of men what was the fuckin' point? Know how many cigarette butts I picked up? I don't even fucking smoke. I mean, what's it matter if the measurement of my ribbon placement isn't perfect on my uniform if I keep my fuckin' weapons in immaculate goddamn order?" I paused but she didn't have an answer. No one had an answer that didn't reek of bullshit. "I got tired of not being treated like a man."

She looked confused. "What do you mean?"

I pointed to a fat guy at another table. "Me and lard-o over there are in the same unit. He goes out and gets a DUI, everyone in the company gets called back in like we were babysitting him and let it happen. No one was personally accountable for shit. Everyone was accountable. So I get in combat we all have to look after each other because no one else is gonna. But back in the rear, back home, what it boils down to is No One is a man. Just cogs in a bullshit machine to be punished when the weakest fucks up whether we had anything to do with it or not. Now they'll say 'the Army isn't about mass punishment,' but that's bullshit in a way. No, it's not about mass punishment; it's more insidious than that. It's about covering your ass. It's so a light colonel can look to the colonel and say 'Private Dipshit fucked up, but I've instructed all my company commanders to call in their companies in the event of an incident to reiterate safety standards.' Blah Blah Blah. Instead of hammering the fuck out of the offender, we all pay for it so an asshole above you can have their ass covered. All it ever did was remind me that I wasn't a man."

I bit into my steak and chewed slowly before looking into her bottomless eyes. "Had they kept me deployed I'd have never left. But I don't guess anyone ever joins up thinking being home would be worse than going to war. But war's easy, it's clear. You know the point of it."

"And you were good at it?" she asked quietly.

I sipped my wine. "I'd like to think so." I crammed a handful of house fries in my mouth and chewed. "What was the day to day with the Order like?"

"Purposeful."

I chuckled. "What's that like?"

She smiled. "Everything was done in the context of a greater good. Life was about a service. There's something gratifying to being part of something greater than yourself."

I nodded. "I get that. I miss 82nd some days."

We sat in silence for a while broken only by the sound of cutlery on bone china.

"So," I finally asked, "what's your mom like?"

She sat a while, chewing longer than she had to in order to buy some time. "Driven."

I sat for a minute. "She hates me, doesn't she?"

Gretchen smiled sadly then slowly nodded. "She'll hate you because of me, not you."

"That's comforting." I managed to smirk, "Is she a ninja like you?"

Her head bobbed. "All the Sisters in Shadow are."

"That's comforting, too."

She laughed and shrugged.

"Anything we can do to deal with things like today?" I watched her dusky features darken as I asked.

She slowly shook her head. Her hair looked like it had bands of blue as the light bounced off the soft ebony waves. "We deal with it one day at a time."

That was life, I guess. "Are they after you or me?"

"Huh?" she asked.

"Are they trying to bring you back in? Or are they trying to get the Sword?"

She took a bite and was really good at milking that excuse to buy time. And when she finally answered it was incredibly useful. "Yes."

I finished my steak and sat for a moment watching her. Then I laughed.

"What?" she asked.

"The Devil's Dipshit Nephew is dating the Preacher's Daughter."

She laughed, and that was always a good thing. "After a dinner this fancy you expecting me to put out?" She smiled.

"Expecting? I'm always expecting you to leave and never come back because that would make sense. You sticking around is borderline insanity." I smirked. "So expecting you to put out, no. Hoping…."

She smiled as the word lingered.

Chapter Fifteen: The Home of Dr. Eric Travis Phenomenal Douche

Anything by Limp Bizkit or Nickleback

Getting into the building was easy. I jumped to the second floor and pulled myself onto a balcony. I opened the door by yanking on it hard enough to break the lock.

We'd watched the side of the building for an hour and a half and knew the apartment was empty. I dug through some drawers and found some mail and learned the occupants were named Douglas, or they were stealing the Douglas's mail anyway. I went to the building's landline and called the security desk and told them I was expecting three guests and to let them up when they got here. I then texted Gretchen "Douglas."

I left the apartment and met Gretchen, Switch and The Grand Vizier Megatron Terabyte the Cyber Samurai. The only reason I'd agreed to this hare-brained bullshit was she promised to go by Tara and dress like a normal fucking person as opposed to her usual Japanophile fuckup.

Gretchen was in a black skirt, white blouse and black jacket hiding some throwing stars and her ASPs. Switch was wearing a black suit, white shirt and pale blue tie with matching pocket square. Tara was in a cream blouse and red skirt and didn't have wacky geisha makeup so really I had nothing to complain about. She was almost unrecognizable without the makeup and wig.

I knew Switch had a Glock 19 under his jacket, and I had my 1911 and my Springfield XDS .45 as a backup. Between Switch, Gretchen and me we knew we would be able to handle any trouble. My worry was Tara going full retard without any warning. We headed up to the eighth floor and didn't have any trouble finding Doc Eric's apartment. The door was open and operatic music was playing. It didn't feel classy as much as it felt like *I'm playing Carmen on vinyl so people know how interesting and cultured I am*.

Tara clung to Switch's arm even though she was taller. Gretchen and I held hands and we slid inside to the open loft with clumps of mingling people. Switch immediately went to where wine was being served. Gretchen walked around the perimeter looking at the art and other decoration on the wall.

Gretchen took a finger sandwich from a passing tray and I found a glass of red wine without having to talk to anyone. The entire apartment felt artificial. It didn't feel like anything was there because people enjoyed it, but was placed there so visitors could see that specific brands had been bought.

"What?" I asked as Gretchen made a face.

She looked up and near-whispered, "The *feng shui* of this place is terrible. The energy flow is so disjointed and weak." I must have made a face because she asked, "What?"

"Everything you just said made me want to break this glass and stab myself in the fuckin' neck with it."

She laughed like I was kidding and I knew enough to let that slide.

The entire place had the feel of someone trying to hard to show how cultured they were. It wasn't a couch; it was a sofa with some designer's name attached to it. It wasn't a chair; it was a handmade artisanal piece. It wasn't a story; it was an attempt to make me kill myself.

I looked around at the people and found a combination of Yuppie Toolbag, Shithead Ignorant Academic, and Hipster Pieces of Shit. This was not a crowd I mixed well with. Gretchen smiled and split off from me to go mingle with some ladies who were discussing how the artist who created the vase was making some kind of representation of a vagina. All I saw was a fucking vase, and an ugly one at that.

I set the wine glass on a passing tray and reached in my pocket pulling out my flask. I unscrewed the cap and took a long sip of the Macallan.

"What are you drinking?"

I turned and saw a lady in a Sari, but the lady was whiter than I was and as ginger as the garnish for sushi. "The Macallan."

"What's that?" she asked curiously.

I took another slug from the flask before screwing the top back and sliding it in my pocket. "It's Scotch."

"But there's wine?" She held up her glass as if I were unaware.

"That's right." God, I just wanted her to walk away.

"Then"—she seemed confused, like a devout nun in a sex shop confused, not a porno nun—"why drink Scotch?"

I stared at her for a moment. Sometimes you can make a snap decision. She and I were never going to be friends. "I drink Scotch to make the rest of you interesting."

Her jaw dropped and her eyes went wide. People always say they want people to be honest, but that's bullshit. People want people to be agreeable, not honest. People want people to be polite, not honest. Honesty is looking at a new mother and saying "Statistically your newborn is insignificant much less special." Honesty is saying "Yes, you do look fat in that, you look fat in everything because you're fat." I'm convinced any woman who asks "Do I look fat in this" knows the answer already, what they're looking for is the pretty lie. People prefer the pretty lie to honesty. Honesty is severely over-fucking-rated.

"Well, I never..." she stated.

I interrupted her. "Dressed like that, short of finding some dude with a weird fetish, I'm not surprised."

She walked away in a huff. I realized I'd probably fucked everything up at this point. The whole concept of a low profile had been shot to hell. It did feel good though. But good feelings didn't pay the bills.

I lucked out though; all attention was on Switch as he was getting into a heated discussion with a guy I would have called a Tool Bag, except for the fact that tool bags are useful.

He was that gangly type of tall that were he a character in a cartoon about men stranded on an island his hallucinating friend would see him as a hot dog, and a weak hot dog at that. He had straight blonde hair which was pomaded to his scalp, not because he liked it that way but because it looked retro; even though it made him look like he was about to betray the von Trapp family in the convent. He had round wire-frame glasses, which he wore because John Lennon was such a poet; *Imagine* was just the communist manifesto put to strings. Admittedly I was an asshole in grade school, but those glasses on that weaselly face just made me want to snap those wireframes and roll the prick for his lunch money. He wore a blazer over a T-shirt for some band I didn't recognize and jeans. I just assumed a person with that level of douche had to be Eric Travis.

It's a simple rule in life. Never trust someone you refer to with all three names or a person with two first names. A person referred to by all three names was an assassin. A person with two first names was at best a jackass and at worst an untrustworthy fuck. This douchebag was the later. From the look of him, he'd never be cool enough to be an assassin.

What the argument between Switch and Doc Douchebag did was provide was a distraction. I slipped out of the large loft room and down a hallway poking my head into doors. I did find the master bedroom illuminating. Paintings depicting the Hell of Dante's *Inferno*, all the literature you'd expect spanning the gamut from *Paradise Lost* to papers on "The inherent patriarchy of Judeo-

Christian and Islamic religious texts" and a lovely Etsy-worthy pentagram dream catcher.

So from that alone I was convinced that Dr. Eric Travis Ph.D. was a demon worshiper, the low thread count of his sheets sealed the deal. I snapped pictures with my phone of all the art, the bookcases, and the papers that were out. Who knew what kind of clues might be found in it all later?

What I didn't find was the Spear we were looking for. That would have been really convenient. Then again had I found it that would have been suspiciously convenient. I preferred to think of myself as a realist, but deep down most realists come off as pessimistic.

But I made sure to snap photos and headed out of the room. I ran into Gretchen in the hall. "Find anything?"

She gestured to the bathroom. "The guy has a collection of artisanal soaps but only buys one-ply toilet paper that feels like quality control rejects from a sandpaper plant."

I couldn't help but smirk. "You know it's the combination of your coy ladylike demeanor and gracious aplomb that constantly drew me to you."

She smiled sweetly. "Bull, it's the facts that I both smell nicer than Switch and Jammer, and I have sex with you on the reg."

I shrugged. I didn't see a reason to argue with gospel-caliber truth.

It was about this time I heard Switch's voice boom from the main room. "You actually believe that there's a white wine under the vast firmament of heaven that compares to a red? I'll drink Spanish sherry and piss in a damn glass to give you white wine."

We slid back into the main room and Gretchen leaned close and whispered, "I kinda feel like that was a line a beer drinker pitched for an episode of 'Fraser.'"

"Switch knows two things," I whispered. "Explosives and red wine."

She giggled then gestured around the room. "Would you ever consider a place like this?"

"No." There was no hesitation in my response. It was as reflexive as your leg jerking when the doctor hits your knee with the little rubber hammer.

I felt her squeeze my arm and her head rest on my shoulder. "Good."

That was comforting.

I laughed and that got the attention of the idiot Sari lady. Why the hell was she wearing a Sari? Did she think it made her cultured or eclectic? I'm generally not a fan of violence against women but if I heard some guy punched that lady in the face my first response wouldn't be "Oh, no, that's terrible" but "Was it an Indian dude?" Because that guy might be owed a shot or two.

Switch pointed to a bottle rack against the wall that seemed more decorative than functional. He walked over and pulled a bottle. "California." He grabbed another bottle. "California." Then a third. "California." He grabbed a fourth. "Arizona."

He looked at the bottle in his hands then looked to the wannabe Nazi-looking hipster. "ARIZONA?" He angrily pushed the bottle back in the rack. "I'm out." He turned and started striding for the door.

Tara moved to join him but stopped and pointed to a bookcase. "Your Full Metal Alchemist is in English." She shook her head in disappointment. "*Arigato*."

The room was relatively silent as she passed the threshold. This left Gretchen and I standing by the hallway alone in Dr. Douchebag's apartment. To be fair this wasn't the first time one of our plans fell apart; then again, in all reality, it probably wouldn't be the last time either.

"I thought he was supposed to be level headed?" Gretchen whispered in the awkward quiet.

"Everyone's got a berserker button, I guess." I must have said that loud enough because several people looked over to us. You could see them doing the mental calculation of "Do I know this person?"

Shit.

I met their eyes and shrugged. "Arizona's a great state, I don't know what that dude's problem was. I mean, they filmed 'Breaking Bad' there."

"That was New Mexico," Gretchen corrected me.

"Oh," I shrugged to the crowd of growing eyes. "Well, aliens and shit."

"That's still New Mexico." Gretchen squeezed my arm.

"Well, Denver's got some great microbreweries." I offered as an olive branch.

"That's Colorado."

As sinister as a group of yuppie hipsters could be, these guys really seemed to crank the creepy up to eleven.

I sighed. "I completely fucked this up, didn't I?"

Gretchen nodded. "Yep."

Chapter Sixteen: There's No Justice

Anthem of the Angels by Breaking Benjamin

I felt Gretchen slide behind me from my right side to my left.
She knew I was a righty and if I had to draw my pistol from under my
left arm she'd need to be clear. What's the sexiest quality a lady
could possess? It's situational awareness. I felt her hand slip into the
crook of my left arm and I looked to the crowd putting on my most
charming of fake smiles.

"Well." I gave a quick wave of my right hand. "We'll be going
now."

"Who are you two?" asked a rather severe-looking lady a gold
stud in her nose that clashed with her matronly gray bun.

I looked to Gretchen then reached into my jacket with my right
hand. I felt my fingers brush my pistol. I drew my hand from under
the jacket and opened the black wallet flashing a gold badge and
identification. "I'm Detective Mickey Linehan and this is Dinah
Brand." I gestured with my head to Gretchen.

Paved with Good Intentions

Some eyes went wide.

Here's the thing. I was taking advantage of three simple facts of existence. First off, most people are sheep and just take the word of an authority figure, whether real or perceived. Secondly, there are so many cop-show procedural and movies on the TV and silver screen that you could throw up pretty much any acronym and you either might hit on some real agency, or at least sound like your a member of a real thing. Federal Bureau of Investigation (FBI), National Reconnaissance Office (NRO), Bureau of Alcohol, Tobacco, Firearms, and Explosives (ATF), and Governor's Taskforce For Illegal Distribution of Pornography to Minors and other Protected Groups, or the GTFIDPMPG. I had made up the last one, but it sounded official, didn't it? It didn't have to be real; it just had to sound like it could be real. Lastly, unless you live in New York or Los Angeles, no one really knows what their city's police badges REALLY looked like in anything other than the abstract.

So all you'd need to pull off looking like a cop is a cheap suit—check—and a hunk of gold looking metal to be a badge—check—and the balls to pull off the lie. Granted impersonating a police officer was a felony, but would we really have been more screwed by that or the sticky wicket we found ourselves?

I snapped the wallet shut and stuffed it back in my jacket pocket, letting Sari lady get a glimpse of the pistol in the under-arm rig. You could tell from her eyes she was going to tell people later that she was in the room with a cop brandishing an AR and was lucky to be alive. I decided to give her a few seconds of the mean mug before glaring at the rest of the people in the room.

"Who is the owner of this place?" I asked glaring officially.

The man with the blonde pomaded hair stepped forward. "I'm Doctor Travis," he said with all the haute and pomp as he could muster.

"Well, good for you." I let my voice ooze sarcasm; it wasn't a huge leap that required any training in the dramatic arts. "Well, congrats you just ruined a seven-damn-month investigation."

"Jesus Christ, I bet you have no idea just how much paperwork alone got flushed down the toilet!" barked Gretchen. God love her, she was playing the part even though no one had given either of us a script.

Dr. Travis looked taken aback and confused. "What, what's going on here?"

I pointed out the door. "That guy who just walked out was a guest of the Douglas's, but what really matters is that that was Maxwell 'Whisper' Thaler!"

"Whisper Freaking Thaler!" Gretchen angrily scolded, letting her voice go high. She was normally sweet as sugar but God she turned the bitchy ire up for the part and it was awesome. She stepped forward and rammed her fingers into his chest eliciting an *oomph*. "If someone dies because you—"

I stepped up and grabbed her shoulder. "Brand, calm down. Get your shit together! Let's go." We started to the door. "Maybe we can catch him."

We moved toward the door and Gretchen looked back and aimed a knife hand at the Douchebag Ph.D. "I swear to God I'll tell the commissioner who fouled this entire operation up. And if Thaler gets away, and I have to tell Foley's widow there's no justice I will wreck you."

I pulled Gretchen into the hallway and she looked up to me and smiled. She half-skipped as we made our way to the stairs instead of waiting for the elevator. God love her, she didn't laugh till the heavy fire door closed behind us.

"Well," she tried catching her breath, "that could have gone better."

I shrugged. "We didn't kick the shit out of a bunch of hipster assholes and ivory tower fuck-nuts so it definitely could have gone worse."

She grinned and nudged my arm. "Look at you being the optimist."

I arched an eyebrow. "Maybe you're rubbing off on me."

She shot me a coy look that seemed dirty, "You're not going to throw a joke about rubbing one out?"

I shook my head.

"Why did you go with Mickey Linehan and not Dick Foley?" she asked curiously.

I shrugged. "Well, I wanted to use The Continental Operative, but he didn't have a name to steal. Dick Foley walked off when he thought the Op might be a murderer. Mickey was faithful to his friend though. So I went with that."

"Plus," she added with a smile, "Foley was Canadian, wasn't he?"

I laughed. "Yeah, fuck that."

She squeezed my arm as we headed down the stairs. "You and your All-American spirit."

"Airborne," I smirked, "All the Way." You could take the private investigator out of the Airborne Rifle Company but you couldn't do the reverse, I guess.

Instead of coming out in the lobby we came out in the alley. He headed down the block toward where Jammer was sitting in a panel van that seemed to scream "People Get Raped In Here!" The only thing that would make it look more like a rape van would be someone spray painting on the sides "Free Candy." Oddly enough, it was so suspicious that no one paid any attention to it.

I opened up the door and Jammer sat there smiling eating from a bag of Funyuns. "Sup?"

I looked around the van. In a movie, it would have been filled with tech gear and monitors. This just had Jammer on a beanbag with a phone and a laptop next to him. He was wearing cut off BDU shorts and a T-shirt advertising a seafood place using a rather disgusting innuendo. Then my eyes fell on what was sitting next to him.

"Jammer?" I asked as Gretchen stood to the side blocking the view. "What the fuck is that?"

He looked next to him confused. "The M-60 Echo?"

"Yes, Jammer, the M-60 Echo." I nodded and felt like I must have looked like the annoyed parent asking questions he already knew the answers to.

"It's an M-60 Echo." Jammer crammed another Funyun in his mouth crunching loudly.

"Why," I said, fighting to not sound pissed, "do you have a goddamn cut-down M-60?"

His face darkened and he spoke in the most reasonable of manners even though it was unreasonable subjects. "Well, last time you got an automatic weapon and I was stuck with a pump shotgun. I just figured, you know, it was my turn."

I sighed. "Okay, don't get pulled over. Where did Switch and Megatron go?"

"I saw them head the other way and hop in a cab. We're meeting for dinner at *Larry's*." Jammer gestured with a Funyun.

I nodded. "Okay, we're gonna swing by the office and we'll meet you guys there."

"Right-O, Daddy-O," he said cheerfully as I slammed the door of the van.

Gretchen and I started walking and I heard the van start behind us. I looked back and waved to Jammer as he pulled up even with us. He rolled the window down.

"For the love of God, don't get pulled over with that thing in the back," I admonished, as I saw Funyun grease smear on the black Bakelite-looking steering wheel.

"The M-60 Echo?" Jammer asked, obviously confused between the cut-down machine gun in the back and the laptop.

"Yes, the goddamned Pig-Gun," I assured him.

He gave a mocking Boy Scout salute and drove away.

Gretchen and I walked and turned the corner to get out of the line of sight of the apartment building.

"Do we have a plan now?" Gretchen asked. There was nothing bitchy or testy about her tone, which is what life had taught me to expect when a lady asked that exact question. Gretchen was refreshing.

"Ish?" Sometimes it doesn't pay to lie and honesty is the best policy. Plus lying to Gretchen never seemed to work out. Maybe it was because we were soulmates but she always seemed to see through my fibs, fabrications, stories, and lies.

"Care to define 'ish?'" she asked with a playful smile.

"Well, I have an idea," I said but added with all honesty.,"but it's not a good one."

We walked a block, there was a bum sitting on some newspaper with a sign that I didn't read. There was no point; they were all the same. Gods love, just need help, need food, vet, blah blah blah. I only had ever read one sign from a bum that I respected. It read "I just want to get fucking drunk and forget." I gave that guy the two crumpled bills and whatever change I had in my pocket. Who knows if he bought booze with it or a sandwich, but I like to hope he got drunk and forgot for a while.

The guy Gretchen and I passed didn't get a second look from me. I got all the sympathy in the world for a guy trying to help himself, but a guy asking for a handout could fuck off. I get I was cold and uncaring but so was the world. There were days I was barely hanging on.

"Want to share?" Gretchen asked and for a moment I thought she was referring to the bum. I glanced back at him and she laughed. "The plan, dummy."

"The plan?" I asked as I stepped over a suspicious puddle on the sidewalk.

She nodded as she seemed to dance over it without ever missing a step.

"We can talk about it at the office," I assured her as she squeezed my arm and leaned her head against my shoulder for a moment.

"Oh?" She sounded curious and excitedly so on top of that.

I laughed. "Yeah, let's not talk about felonies in public."

"Like your fake badge?" she purred; her voice held a dangerous feline quality to it.

I chuckled. "Yeah, like the fake badge and all the other fake IDs I got on me."

"What other IDs?" She half-jumped as she asked.

"Well, I got a couple of union cards, reporter credentials, stuff like that." UAW card was in the back left pocket, reporter credentials were in my right jacket pocket, and set of fake power company credentials were in my back right pocket. You never knew what lie you'd have to tell whom or when.

"Well, that's wily of you." She stepped closer as we walked and reached down interlacing her fingers in mine. "How often have you used them?"

"That was my first time playing the cop." I said with a small grin.

"Well, good job not saying Sam Spade, that might have been too obvious," she congratulated me as she rubbed my knuckle with her thumb.

"Well, good on you for following along."

"Were you worried?" she asked demurely.

"Not for a second," I assured her.

She laughed. "You are not that good a liar, Nick Decker."

Chapter Seventeen: Larry's

Eat It **by Weird Al Yankovic**

I was convinced that at some point Larry's had been a strip club. When you first entered it was into a small anteroom with a window that you would have paid your cover through, had there been a cover. Instead, this was where your ID was checked, and T-shirts, mugs, key chains, and other things I couldn't understand why anyone would want to buy could be bought.

The place had a bare concrete floor that was probably easy to clean. The bar was against the back wall. There was a stage to the left as you came in that I was convinced once had an island coming out into the main room for stripping. Now the island was gone but the stage was set up for a band or a comedian or a juggler or whatever passed for entertainment. There were four pool tables possessing varying quality of felt. It was a place of mismatched stools and tall tables, and a few tables with six seats. It looked like a bar that should have been a biker bar, but no bikers had claimed it.

Instead what you had in attendance were lower-middle class and cleaner blue collar workers who were just looking for an escape.

To some couples Larry's was a night out; I couldn't tell if that was a fact to find comforting or sad.

A jukebox sang in the corner, playing hits of the eighties and nineties. I enjoyed, for the most part, and Gretchen bore it in good humor even though she seemed more a product of my decades than her own generation. She was at least fifteen years younger than me. I was pushing forty and she wasn't quite mid-twenties. Yet I never really thought about it. She didn't strike me as one of the kids the rest of the people her age seemed to be. Maybe it was because I'd seen her throw down and shoot people. Maybe it was because I'd taken the time to get to know her at all. Maybe it was because she was my soulmate. Maybe it was because she was a total smoke show. Who the fuck knows?

Larry was three hundred pounds and a sixth that age. He held onto the illusion of hair with the wispy halo of frazzled silver that no amount of tending could tame; even though his scalp still seemed to show through it all. His beard was the type Gandalf would masturbate thinking about. It almost seemed like the hair had stopped growing from the top of his head and simply let gravity pull it out of his face. He would stroke it lovingly the way Ernst Stavro Blofeld would stroke his cat.

He wore an orange puffy vest like Marty McFly wore in *Back to the Future*. Not because he was trying to be nostalgic, but just because it was comfortable and he liked it. He wore a pair of cut off khakis that I'm convinced were what he wore the day he walked away from a desk job and bought a strip club to turn it into a bar and them sliced off at the knees with a pair of kids' safety scissors.

Larry had always adamantly denied that the place had been a strip club with the same fanatical vehemence of an Auschwitz guard in his belief he'd done nothing wrong and was just following orders.

I scanned the room as Gretchen and I came in. Gretchen had changed into a pair of tight yoga pants, her pouch belt with throwing stars and other sundries, a gray tank top, her leather half-jacket, and her highly polished jungle boots. I was still in my dark gray suit and black and white Chucks. I wouldn't say we drew looks as we came through the door, but she did. She always did.

I scanned the room and found Switch and Tara bravely holding down one of the larger tables from encroachment from any of the other patrons. I walked over toward them as Gretchen went over to the bar to put in an order. I wouldn't recommend the food at Larry's to anyone with one massive exception: the meatball sub. The bread was soft on the inside but crunched on the golden brown outside with each bite. There was a mix of mozzarella and provolone cheeses, but not so much cheese that it becomes disgusting. The meatballs were homemade daily with the bread. The meatballs were fried up in a skillet then tossed to stew in homemade marinara. The kicker was the bread would be sliced along the top, then the trench lined with large slices of deli pepperoni and hard salami before the meatballs and marinara were added. The meats helped keep the bread from becoming soggy with anything but grease. Then the entire sandwich was tossed in a broiler to brown and bubble the cheese. Apparently Larry's wife Isabella and sister-in-law Maria traded their abilities to cook anything else in this life to create the perfect sandwich. Somehow, on top of all that, they sold them for only five bucks.

Gretchen smiled as she threw in our sandwich orders to Larry, who always appreciated the attention of lovely young ladies. They say the quickest way to a man's heart is under the left shoulder and in with a long, thin stiletto-like blade, taking care to wiggle it around a lot for good measure. Secondbest is in and up under the floating ribs. But the third best way is probably with food. She paid with a stack of crumpled one-dollar bills that probably had spent more time crumpled in the edge of a thong than most bills ever would.

Gretchen glided her way across the room with the grace of a professional dancer or waitress. I laughed as I heard one of the guys in the bar look to Gretchen and remark, "I bet her snatch is like a damn cigar cutter." I didn't say anything. On the one hand, I get its objectifying and not kosher, on the other hand, I dunno. I know Gretchen can fight her own battles though and I don't get in the way of it. Not that I guess anyone is going to look at me and say, "Wow, I bet his dick could hold up a mailbox." It couldn't, not even on my best day.

I got to the table and saw Switch and Megatron sharing a basket of fried pickles with ranch dipping sauce. I grimaced; I didn't like pickles anyway much less fried. Even though most things were better fried.

"Did no one tell you about the sandwiches?" I asked as I pulled a seat to plop in.

"What sandwiches?" Switch asked.

I gestured to the plastic menu on the table. "This place makes the best damn meatball sub, man."

Switch sighed and rubbed the bridge of his nose. "See, meatball sandwiches are either amazing or shit."

"Well, they're phenomenal here," I assured him.

"What's phenomenal?" Gretchen asked as she took a chair next to me. "The meatball sandwiches?"

Switch seemed to shoot her a look that seemed to weep "*Et tu, bro?*"

"There's gonna be a band tonight," Megatron chimed in, a little too perky.

"Great," I said with none of the enthusiasm that the word deserved.

"You don't like live bands?" Switch asked.

"Nick doesn't like anything." Megatron laughed a laugh that dripped accusation and derision. It hurt a little when Gretchen laughed as well.

Switch leaned back. "Some things never change."

"What's that supposed to fucking mean?" I glared at my old Army buddy that I had hoped would take my side if the girls were ganging up on me.

Switch drummed his fingers on the table. "We're in camped outside of Fallujah, and Nick here goes off one day on the cooks."

Gretchen looked confused. "Nick's usually pretty nice to wait-staff."

Megatron took the confused look baton and ran with it. "When is Nick nice to anyone?"

"He's nice to people he figures could spit in his food," Gretchen explained with an extreme tone oozing politick and everyone at the table accepted the logic of it.

I looked at Switch. "Bro, you left a lot out of that story."

"Well," Tara half sneered—I think she was intentionally trying to get under my skin—"fill in the gaps."

"Well, sure," I said leaning back and crossing my arms. "I went off on the cooks; except for the fact they weren't fucking cooking anything. They were just dishing out of marmites that came from the next camp over. Then, they weren't even dishing it, they were pulling KPs from the rifle companies, and they weren't cleaning anything because they were making the KPs do that too. So those worthless pieces of shit weren't doing anything but rat-fucking the snacks that came over and none of the good shit ever getting to us. And on top of all that, we'd had boiled fucking chicken for ninety-six goddamned days straight." I stopped and let that sink into the mostly uncomprehending ears of Megatron Terabyte. "So yeah, I made an exception to my normal policy in terms of dealing with food service personnel and went the fuck off on some cooks."

Switch laughed and slapped his knee. "It was great. You had a piece of shit cook E7 going off on how hard their job is. Nick here takes a box of MREs and throws it at him. Just slings the box at him and yells '*I ghosted four motherfuckers yesterday! What the fuck did you do?*'" He laughed so hard he had to wait till he caught his breath. "Then Nick here starts walking off and the guy says something and Nick looks back, knife-hands the guy and growls, literally growls, '*I hope the world goes to shit so I get the chance to let you die, you worthless wad of pond scum ejaculate.*'" He laughed again and then grimaced as he ate one of the fried pickles. "I mean who can come up with that?"

Gretchen laughed and leaned her head affectionately on my shoulder. "So, what happened?"

"Nothing." I shrugged and looked down into her upturned eyes. "I finished that tour and did one more, that one in Afghanistan. Then I got out."

"And the cook," Switch added with mock sincerity, but was probably too accurate in reality to be comforting, "is probably a retired sergeant major now talking about how hard he was back in Fallujah when shit was real."

It got somber for a moment but that was killed when I heard the loud gregarious voice explode behind me. "Nicolai?"

I felt the smile tug unbidden but completely warranted to my face. I didn't even have to look back as I waved over my shoulder. "Hey, Yuri."

The sound of Yuri's feet pounded across the concrete floor and I felt his big meaty paw grab and shake my shoulder. "Nicolai, my friend. You come for sandwich, no?"

I reached up and patted Yuri's hand. "You know me too well, Yuri. You?"

"Yes," he boomed, "sandwich very good."

I gestured to Switch and Megatron. It was apparent from the look on Switch's face that he was thinking about the sandwich. "Yuri, this is my good friend Switch.,"—Switch stood and clasped hands with Yuri, or should I say Yuri's hand engulfed his—"and that's Tara."

Yuri reached across the table and shook Tara's hand, and my, he shook; I mean nearly tore her arm out of socket.

"This is my wife, Mary Jo," Yuri beamed with pride as he pulled his wife forward. "This" was pronounced "dis." Mary Jo was wearing her red-and-white checked pattern dress that had a Laura Ingles Wilder feel, but instead of seeming silly it really fit her and her curly locks.

I smiled up to Mary Jo. "Tough day in the ER, Mary Jo?"

The nurse smiled. "There was a little drama, but when isn't there?" She reached over and roughed the top of my hair like she was a coach and I just made a great play. "But it's always good to see you, Nick."

I slid my arm around Gretchen and gave her a squeeze. "Mary Jo, have you met Gretchen?"

Mary Jo beamed. "No, I haven't but Yuri told me you had a girlfriend!"

Gretchen hopped up and held her arms open. "I'm Gretchen, and I'm a hugger!"

"Me too!" Mary Jo squealed and wrapped her arms around Gretchen's shoulders. They both seemed to bounce as they hugged and neither Yuri nor I could stop from smiling.

I saw Jammer coming over wearing his date suit and had Joy with an E-Y on his arm. Jammer laughed, as he got close. "Hey, Yuri, didn't know you were coming to the party."

Yuri slapped Jammer's shoulder and shook his hand. "We come for the music. Mary Jo big, big fan."

I raised my eyebrow and glanced at the stage where people were starting to set up amps and a drum kit. "Who's playing?"

Mary Jo laughed and hugged Joy as Gretchen introduced her. Tara had gotten up and joined the crowd of ladies as Yuri and Jammer both sat at the table with Switch and me.

"Mary Jo!" Yuri boomed in the way you imagine Santa Claus laughing, "What name of band playing?"

"*Streetlight People.*" She laughed and Joy with an E-Y gasped and started bouncing with excitement.

I shook my head in resignation. "Goddamnit."

Chapter Eighteen: Streetlight People

Don't Stop Believing by Journey

The drummer was a chubby, balding guy in his mid-forties who after two minutes under the lights would be drenched in sweat despite wearing jogging pants and a vest. The keyboardist had a piercing in each nostril, in her left eyebrow, and a ring in her lip. Her make up would have been garish in 1987. She had a six-inch faux-hawk and this sides of her head were almost shorn off but what was there was dyed bright orange. She looked to be in her mid-twenties and took her "music" or "craft," or whatever artsy people called it, seriously.

The bassist looked bored, and from the generic nature of his outfit was probably in several other bands, hoping one made it. The rhythm guitarist had a mullet, and beyond that deserved no attention. The lead guitarist was female, early thirties, but obviously wished she'd been a teenager in the late eighties or early nineties. Ripped-up, stone-washed Jordache jeans clung to her legs and she had a denim vest that had once been a jean jacket before she razored off the sleeves and bedazzled the hell out of it. On the back was a bedazzled train with the phrase "Going Anywhere" under it.

The lead singer looked like a high school English teacher, who watched vintage porn and decided to dress like the actors he observed. He wore leather pants, though he really shouldn't have. I couldn't tell if his spiked, white mullet top and straight mullet back were a wig or simply a poor collection of life choices. His gut was not designed for the tank top he had pulled over it. It was a collection of people desperately clinging to a dream that they might have been happier letting go.

Some bands play because they genuinely enjoy it. These guys played because they genuinely, and misguidedly, thought they were going to make it. Some bands play covers and make it because they make their own music. These, with maybe the exception of the keyboardist, played covers and thought they'd make it doing that, just that. It's hard to respect idiots. But before I could really give it more thought my meatball sub arrived.

The sub came, as all subs should, in a plastic basket; mine was red and Gretchen's was blue, lined with deli paper. The sub sat along one end and down the side, the rest of the free space was taken up by a pickle wrapped up in wax paper, a bag of Golden Flake Sweet Heat potato chips, and two small envelopes, one with red pepper flakes and the other with powdered parmesan. I took the wrapped-up pickle and handed it to Gretchen who took it gleefully, unwrapping it and taking a bite before setting it in the basked with her own wrapped-up pickle.

"That does look good," Switch muttered as I lifted half of my sandwich and took a bite from the cut end. The crisp sound of my teeth tearing into the bread could never be described with any onomatopoeic turn of phrase. It was easily the most texturally perfect bite of food under the firmament of heaven. I was pretty sure if God ordered take out meatball subs, he'd get them from Larry's; I knew for a fact that Lucifer enjoyed them.

"Well, go get you one." Gretchen smiled as she bit into her sandwich with that perfect sound of teeth tearing into crisp, but not overly crisped bread that no onomatopoeia could accurately convey. She had a smear of marinara on her cheek. Mary Jo handed her a napkin and Gretchen flushed with embarrassment as she wiped her face before taking another bite and having to repeat the process.

I dug into my sandwich and Yuri walked over squatting between Switch and me. "Nicolai, I have question," he whispered conspiratorially.

"Shoot," I told him around a mouthful of meatball perfection.

"I am not sure, the young lady with Jammer is young lady, truly," Yuri's whisper wasn't out of concern of being overheard by anyone at the table except Mary Jo. He recognized that the subject of conversation would bring a lecture from the sweet lady who decided to marry him.

"That's not a question, Yuri," Switch chuckled before leaning in and whispering, "but he's right, though."

"Well," I whispered, "Jammer knows, so who are we to bitch, right?"

Both Switch and Yuri thought about that for a few seconds then moved back to the chairs. The band was still setting up and Mary Jo, Gretchen, and Megatron all hopped up to run to the jukebox to get one or two more songs in before the band played.

Jammer reached over and grabbed one of the fried pickles and popped it in his mouth with all the care of a pig inspecting his slop.

"Jammer," Yuri said slowly as the girls were out of earshot. "You with girl-boy? Boy-girl? Yuri confused, my friend."

Jammer laughed and reached for another pickle, which he had not offered to help pay for. "Bro, it's awesome."

"Awesome?" Switch asked.

I didn't say anything because I was busy finishing the first half of my sandwich. Opening my bag of Golden Flake Sweet Heat before going after the second half.

"Yeah, man." Jammer smiled, speaking loudly enough to be heard over the crowd and without any sense of shame or care for who heard it. "Yeah, all the bits feel right, I can bang the fucking bottom out of her, without ever using a condom and I'm never"—he held his arms wide like he was telling a fish story—"NEVER going to have to sit through a 'I'm late, we need to talk' conversation."

Switch and Yuri sat back in stunned silence.

"It's fucking foolproof, guys." Jammer laughed and patted his own chest. "Hell, I'm a fool and this is working fucking awesomely."

I bit into a few fingers full of Sweet Heat chips. Watching Switch and Yuri you could see the wheels turning. Both men recognized the logic, but there is a difference between recognizing and accepting logic. Airplanes fly because the shape of the wing creates a low pressure up top and the pressure under the wing lifts it. The science is fairly simple, but there are still plenty of people afraid of flying. Even though I think that's bullshit. I don't think anyone is really afraid of flying; it's the crashing they're afraid of.

Point being Jammer was either a secret genius or a guy who thought Metallica's *St. Anger* was better than *And Justice For All*.

"Joy's cool, guys," I said as I picked up the other half of my sandwich. Over the speakers, we heard the soft beat of music. Then an ethereal whistle that sounded like a flute or some woodwind but was probably a synthesizer.

"What song this?" Yuri asked, giving up on figure out Jammer and Joy.

"*Where the Streets Have No Name,*" Switch said with a distinct lack of confidence.

I shook my head and corrected with a mouthful of meatball sub. "It's U2 but it's *With or Without You*."

Switch seemed unconvinced until Bono started singing. Then he sighed and slumped in his seat. His seat might as well have been named defeat. Then he pushed his chair back. "I'm gonna get one of those sandwiches."

The girls came back and Gretchen sat between Mary Jo and me. Yuri was between Mary Jo and Jammer. Megatron was between Joy with an E-Y and Switch. The table wasn't meant for eight but we were making it work.

After U2 we got The Corrs' *Breathless*. That caused an argument over whether it was The Corrs or the Coors. One was an Irish pop band and one was an American beer brewed in the Rockies. I won't say who was on which side of the argument but it was heated, not quite friendship ending but definitely straining.

Megatron was wrong.

Then the jukebox cut off and we heard the slightly nasally voice come over the speakers causing a squeal before the keyboardist ran out the soundboard and backed off the mic.

"Gentleman and most especially ladies,—that got a halfhearted laugh and an over-enthusiastically voluminous cheer from the more drunk members of the audience—"We are Streetlight People, and we are happy to have you with us and hope you join us on our Journey."

I normally like puns, but that one made me want to open my veins and end it all, if not just outright suck-starting a pistol.

The band opened with *Wheel in the Sky*. Mary Jo got up and pulled Yuri to his feet. They started dancing out in the open floor. Yuri was spry for a guy his size and age. Mary Jo was the image of awkward. Her dancing was the equivalent to the one lady in a church choir who makes a "joyful noise."

I leaned into the table and gestured everyone closer. "Okay, I got a plan for the Spear."

Jammer smiled and tore into his sandwich savagely.

"Don't want Yuri to hear?" Switch asked.

"I want to keep him out of trouble unless we're fucking desperate." I nodded and I felt Gretchen squeeze my hand under the table. She knew.

"So what's your plan?" Megatron asked like she was part of our team. Joy with an E-Y knew to keep her trap shut in regards to things outside her wheelhouse.

"We're going to kidnap Dr. Douchebag." I knew I could have tried to build it up more. But with the way this band was rushing the music that knew when *Wheel in the Sky* would end.

Jammer nodded yes as he took another bite of sandwich. Switch thought about it for a moment, weighed the pros and cons in his head then with raised eyebrows nodded his ascent.

"That's your plan!" Megatron gasped.

I ignored her and looked to Gretchen. "We'll use the van we stashed." She smiled and gave me a sure nod. I looked at Switch. "I'm gonna need some thermite to fist-fuck his engine and scare him out of his car." Switch laughed and rubbed his hands together with a maniacal glee. I then looked to Jammer. "We're gonna need a black site."

He thought and crammed some chips in his mouth, flecks ending up in his beard. "How black?"

"Pretty black."

"Dramatic or functional?" Jammer added chips to his face hole like he was a kid feeding quarters to a Dig Dug machine.

"This guy is a dipshit, so go dramatic." I watched the gleam of mischief shine in Jammers eyes as I added, "You're off the fucking leash, bro."

"When are we doing this?" Switch asked practically.

"Tomorrow on his way to work." It wasn't a long timeline, but really kidnapping this shit head didn't seem like that hard a job.

"What's the breakdown?" Jammer inquired as he reached over for some of Joy with an E-Y's disgusting chili cheese fries.

"Gretchen and I are the snatch team." I then gestured between Switch and Jammer. "Then you two grab and go. We meet at the black site and figure out where this shit is. Bing, bang, boom, done."

The band broke into *Anyway You Want It*. Gretchen jumped up and ran over cutting in and dancing with Yuri. Mary Jo came back with a laugh. I watched, no one on that dance floor moved like Gretchen.

Gretchen and Joy with an E-Y danced with Switch during *Lights*. Joy with an E-Y and Jammer did some kind of pre-fuck ritual during *Lovin', Touchin', Squeezin'*. Frankly, that was a little disturbing to watch. Mary Jo, Yuri, Switch, and Megatron had some group dance thing going during *Only The Young*.

I got roped into dancing with Mary Jo during *Open Arms*. It was middle school rules. Mary Jo was just happy to be there with friends. "Yuri thinks of you as a little brother, you know?" she confessed.

I chuckled. "I think of him as my second coolest uncle."

That got a laugh from her. "He's not the coolest?"

"You've not met my Uncle Lew."

"He wouldn't tell me about the trouble in a little while ago," Mary Jo said cautiously. I don't think she was intentionally probing. Then again I wasn't going to tell her that her husband had been sniping fools using a Dragunov while Jammer helped me murder a bunch of dipshit Christian Bikers.

"You got a good man there, Mary Jo," I assured her. "Better than most."

She smiled, content with that. "I like Gretchen. She's good for you."

"How so?" I didn't doubt her, I was just curious about the view from the gallery.

"Before, you always seemed lost." She smiled sweetly and looked over to Gretchen. "But not when you're with her."

The song ended and before I could sit Gretchen slid into my arms. I held her and we swayed as Streetlight People did a halfway decent job of playing *Faithfully*.

I was still holding her, many songs later, when the band closed with *Don't Stop Believing*. It wasn't a song you held someone and slow danced to, but we did it anyway.

Chapter Nineteen: A Gearing Up and Team Building Montage

You're the Best by Joe "Bean" Benitez

T he thermite charge that Switch gave me was about the size and shape of a good old-school hardback copy of Charles Dickens's *Tale of Two Cities*. It looked like a bundle wrapped in duct tape with a little box on one of the flat sides with a switch. That was it. No crazy wires and timers and other shit you'd see in a movie. It was pretty innocuous, or at least as innocuous as a homemade incendiary that would melt through the block of a car could be anyway.

Thermite doesn't explode; it burns, really freaking hot. Thermite is what you set on a tank if you want to melt through the armor. In the military we'd have thermite incendiary grenades in our trucks in case they got fucked up we could slag the truck so the bad guys couldn't fix or use it. Now I had a messenger bag over my shoulder holding the MacGyver'ed package Switch had given me.

"All right," he told me as he showed me the device, "you flip the switch and you got two or three seconds before that's going to bore a hole to China."

"Where's the safety?" I asked looking at it, only seeing one toggle on it.

"There isn't one." He seemed confused about the question being asked in the first place.

"So, you're telling me if that fucker gets toggled in the bag it's gonna melt through my back and out my dick?" My tone easily conveyed my displeasure.

"No," he assured me, "it'll burn down out the bottom of the bag melting your ass, the back of your legs and your feet off. The rest of you will just catch on fire."

"That isn't fuckin' reassuring, Switch!"

Jammer laughed, but Gretchen looked concerned.

"Want me to put some tape over it?" Switch offered with conciliatory magnanimity.

"Jesus fuckin' Christ, when did you turn into Rocket fuckin' Raccoon?" My voice had gone higher than I'd preferred. But I did not see a point in hiding my displeasure at the fact that I could be turned into a fiery version of the Wicked Witch of the West.

Gretchen gasped and looked between me, Switch and Jammer. She pointed out Switch. "If he's Rocket, that makes me Gamora." She pointed to me with a huge smile. "Nick is Star-Lord."

"Obviously," I added as she continued.

She looked at Jammer. "So is Jammer Drax The Destroyer or Groot?"

He thought for a moment and then pulled out a can of dip, putting a wad of Grizzly in his lip. "I'm Yondu."

Gretchen scrunched her face in thought. "Why Yondu?"

He smiled and spit on the concrete floor of the warehouse we had stashed the van in and was using as our base for the black site. "Because I'm Nick's Daddy."

Gretchen looked confused. "Isn't Nick older than you?"

"Don't think about it." I smirked to Gretchen before looking to Jammer and assuring him, "I don't need you to pump me up." I signed and lifted my .45 from the table and pressure-checked the slide till I saw the brass of the cartridge in the chamber. I let it slide forward. I thumbed the hammer back and pushed it into my underarm rig, clasping it between the hammer and the slide.

Gretchen was wearing her single action Army custom .357s on her thighs under a longish cape that probably had some designer's name to it, which fell to her knees covering the cartridge belt. The cape was a dark purple, so dark it almost looked black until the light hit it. With the cape covering her shorts and T-shirt, the only other article of clothes you could see was her jungle boots. It didn't take a great imagination to picture her naked under the cape. It didn't take a lot of prompting to, either.

Jammer and Switch were both wearing coveralls the patches of which claimed that their names were "Francis" and "Joey." Jammer was wearing the Joey and for a moment I was wondering if there was a connection between the coveralls and Joy with an E-Y. I was willing to chalk it up to a coincidence and not push the issue.

In addition to the thermite charge, Switch gave both Gretchen and I what looked like a thin sandwich with the bread behind a piece of cardboard and the back an equally sized irregular circle of steel. Sandwiched between them were several wraps of Det-Chord.

"What's the hockey puck for?" Gretchen asked as she twirled it in her dexterous fingers before finding a pouch for it on her belt. She didn't have an empty pouch so she pulled out what I first thought was jacks, then I realized the ends had been sharpened. Gretchen had been carrying around anti-personnel caltrops. Why did I find that fucking hot?

"In case you have to blow the locks on the car door. You know, if he mans up and doesn't bolt when you melt the hood." Switch sounded pretty pleased with himself. He was armed with a Glock 17 and an AK-47. Jammer was carrying his nickel-plated .45 and was slapping a drum magazine onto an AA-12. An AA-12 is a fully automatic 12-gauge shotgun.

"Why wouldn't we just break the windows?" Gretchen asked, and Switch's pleased face dropped with all the surety of gravity.

"Jammer," I asked, "why the fuck do you have an AA-12?"

He looked confused. "Well, you told me I couldn't carry the M-60..."

"And you still can't," I reiterated.

"Well, since it seems like I'm the eternal shotgun guy, I figured why not an automatic one?" He spoke calmly like the concept of him carrying a fully auto 12-gauge was completely reasonable. It was the cool, measured tone of a parent trying to reason with their child to eat their vegetables so they can be strong like Popeye. Jammer then looked to Switch with the AK. "But, bro, you look like a fucking straight-up terrorist."

Gretchen and I both looked to Switch. With his sub-continental features and complexion, and his black-and-gray peppered beard, and the universally assigned rifle for bad guys he did kind of fit the profile for your stereotypical Taliban asshole.

He looked at the AK then he looked to the three of us. You could see the disappointment on his face. "Seriously?"

I shrugged and Gretchen held up her hand giving the wavering palm.

"That's racist," Switch spat.

"Probably," I agreed, "but that doesn't mean it's not fucking accurate."

"I'm glad you dropped out of the Tora Bora Suicide Bomber Academy." Gretchen grinned. "But I bet the graduation party would have been a blast!"

Switch sighed. "From them I expect it." He shook his head and looked to Gretchen. "But you?"

"Sorry," she said with genuine contrition, which seemed to slightly mollify Switch.

"So, what do you want?" Switch asked the group at large.

"Switch, switch guns with Jammer?" Gretchen offered, it took us all a moment to figure out the double Switch in her statement.

"But I look good with this!" Jammer whined as he held up the AA-12 in a very Rambo-like pose as if he were going to hip-fire it.

Switch walked over and took it from him. He handed Jammer the AK and the two of them turned to face Gretchen and me. "Better?" Switch asked.

Gretchen and I both nodded in agreement. "Much," Gretchen assured them.

"What do you want me to do?" Megatron asked from the corner by the shipping container we were going to use for the interrogation space. For the second day in a row, she was dressed like a regular fucking human being.

I'll be honest, in the prep for the op I'd forgotten she was there.

"Keep monitoring the phone bug Gretchen sat in Dr. Douchebag's apartment and let us know when he's on the move."

"Is she part of the team now?" Jammer asked gesturing to Megatron.

"No," I adamantly let everyone know.

"Well, none of us do computer stuff," Jammer mischievously spoke with a look of trouble as his thick eyebrows raised.

"Our cock-to-vagina ratio is becoming kinda skewed," Switch added.

"Hey," I glared at Switch, "you just got on the team. If anyone's throwing the ratio off it's you."

He made a p*shhh* out of the side of his mouth. "I've been on the team since Fallujah."

"He has a point," Jammer agreed.

He did have a point. Knowing someone is right doesn't make it easier to accept sometimes.

Gretchen hugged my arm and looked up with big wet eyes. "I think she's great."

"Your judgment can't be trusted," I told her. "You sleep with me."

Switch and Jammer both nodded in agreement.

"Yeah, Gretchen," Switch said sympathetically, "of all of us your life choices seem the most questionable."

Jammer's head bobbed in agreement. "I mean a blind man could see you could do better than Nick."

"Well, fuck y'all, too," I told two of my oldest friends. But I smiled. Sometimes you couldn't help it around those two. Sometimes you really couldn't help it around those three. A guy like me could never deserve Switch, Jammer, or Gretchen.

"Fuck it," I muttered and turned to look at Tara. "You're on the fucking team."

She narrowed her eyes. "What if I don't want to be on your stupid team?"

I shrugged. "Fine by me."

"Okay, okay, I want to be on the team," she gushed. "I don't have a lot of friends."

"No fucking kidding..." I didn't say more because Gretchen put an elbow in my ribs.

"One condition," Tara added quickly.

I shot her a quizzical look.

She smiled, and it was a mean smile. The type of smile Torquemada probably had when torturing people gave him an erection. It was a smile that would have been at home on Elizabeth Bathory's face while bathing in virgin blood. She smiled the smile of a divorced stripper spending the alimony and child support check her soldier husband just sent on cocaine, body glitter, and her newest boyfriend.

"What's my name?" she asked coyly.

I sighed and felt Gretchen wrap her arm around my waist giving me a caring squeeze.

I looked at the blonde, annoying, wannabe Asian woman. Every word was like a lobotomy probe ramming around my eye and punching into my brain. I was a Randal McMurphy without a Chief to put me out of my misery. "The Grand Vizier Megatron Terabyte the Cyber Samurai."

She giggled. "Doesn't that feel good?"

"I fuckin' hate you," I muttered.

Gretchen squeezed my waist then bounced up to kiss my cheek. "Be nice."

I looked to Jammer and Switch. "Strength and Honor, brothers."

They nodded and replied, "Strength and Honor." We'd stolen it from the movie *Gladiator*, and Ridley Scott had probably stolen it from somewhere else, but for us it was tradition. We reached out and instead of shaking hands grasped each other by the forearm; first me and Switch, and then me and Jammer. Gretchen gave them both hugs.

I laughed. "Smoke me a kipper, I'll be back for breakfast."

Jammer laughed harder and replied, "See you, Space Cowboy."

They loaded in the panel van to head out to the spot where they would wait for the signal. The signal they were looking for being the hood of the car starting to melt and the hot blinding flash of thermite.

I held Gretchen's right hand with my left as we walked to the stolen Chevy Malibu she had boosted from the parking lot of a grocery store. She climbed into the passenger seat and I hopped behind the wheel.

In retrospect, I would have done things differently. I would have said something, done something, anything. But life moves one direction; no pause, instant replay, or rewind. Life was a bad TV show with no editor and the most annoying of commercials.

I would have done something, said something, anything; had I known that moment was going to be the last time the five of us would ever be in the same room again in this life.

Chapter Twenty: SNAFU

Dirty Deeds by AC/DC

SNAFU is an acronym that was born in the military. Marines will say they made it up, and then will return to the business of eating crayons. Sailors will say they created it, just before they go back to performing in the Village People. Army guys will tell you they lost the lease but it definitely was their property, or that it was theirs but they lost it in their second divorce during their third deployment. Within the Army, paratroopers will tell you they may not have created it but they definitely stole it and won't give it back. The Coast Guard will try to say something but no one will pay attention. The Air Force is too young so they have no valid claim on the intellectual property.

SNAFU. No one word could describe our lives with the scientific accuracy of a SNAFU.

Situation
Normal

All

Fucked

Up

I waited in the alley, standing behind a dumpster. I'd taken the thermite charge out of the bag because I kept imagining it melting me in half. Out of the bag, I could look at the switch. I reached under it and pulled off the cover of the command adhesive strip Switch had put there to keep it from sliding off the hood before going off. He'd thought of everything but a goddamned safety.

Switch and Jammer waited in the fan down the block at the other end of the alley. The plan was to box Dr. Douchebag in and herd him to the van. Murphy's Laws of combat dictate "that no plan survives first contact with the enemy." I'm not sure we even made it that far.

Gretchen crashed the Malibu down the block from the alley and traffic was backing up. She moved out of sight and waited until Dr. Douchebag pulled his BMW, which could affectionately be christened the *SS Definitely Making Up For Something*, into the alley. Gretchen followed him into the alley on foot and started to follow him toward me with slow steady steps.

I stepped out from behind the dumpster and wondered for a second if I was about to get flattened because this guy didn't want to break. Luckily for me that BMW had great breaks. I jumped backward to keep my knees from getting bashed in and I slammed my fist in the hood denting it, feeling the power of the sword wanting to manifest.

"I'M WALKING HERE, MOTHERFUCKER!" I roared at the man behind the windshield. He didn't recognize me from the party yet. It was a delicious moment though. Maybe deep down, every guy who has made his living doing gun work, in some form or another is a bully. Maybe I just like thinking I'm Robin Hood sticking it to the Sheriff of Nottingham. But there is something gratifying, satisfying, and a little goddamned endearing to seeing someone who thinks he is important and powerful as he is reminded that he is small and without the protection of civilization is just meat to an apex predator. Some of us wolves don't prey on the flock, but it is nice to remind them, every once in a while, that they are fucking sheep. Dr. Eric Travis Douchebag Ph.D. was quickly realizing his place in a Darwinian structure in which his economics and position meant jack and shit as he looked at the visible dent in the hood of his car.

I felt the rage tickling at the back of my brain and it felt good as I pushed the thermite package to the hood of his car and flipped the switch. I turned my head and looked away as I ducked back behind the dumpster. There was a loud *woooooshhh* behind me and even in the shadow of the dumpster, the light was searing. I pushed my Wayfarers higher up on the bridge of my nose and came around the dumpster. What was left of the hood of the BMW was slag and on fire.

A man of action would have been on the move. Dr. Douchebag was sitting there gripping the steering wheel with white knuckles immovable as Michelangelo's *David*. If he'd not taken his eyes off the package he was probably blind as his ocular nerves were probably shot to hell and burned like a kid's marshmallow over a campfire. I smashed the shatter-resistant glass of the driver's side window with my elbow; I probably couldn't have done that without the power of the sword. I reached through the hole and grabbed him by the collar of his designer suit jacket—who designed it I had no idea—getting a handful of pink polo shirt in the process. Had he been wearing his seat belt I might have had a problem, as it was, I had absolutely no issue yarding that pretentious son of a bitch out of the broken window slinging him from the car causing his back to slam into the wall like a sack of shit.

I turned away from the car and glanced both ways. Gretchen had made it to the trunk of the car, and the other direction the van was blocking the front of the alley. Switch was behind the wheel and Jammer was running toward us with a syringe in his left hand and the AK over his back ready to be slung around to his right hand. The plan was to inject the asshole with ketamine, a painkiller designed for horses, and then wake him up later with a shot of adrenaline to his heart *Pulp Fiction* style.

I saw Dr. Douchebag try to pull himself to his feet. I sprinted as much as you could with only three steps and put my shoulder into him as he wavered, slamming him back into the wall. I need him alive, but broken was still a viable option.

It was then that we heard the simultaneous sounds of screeching tires and a car crash. I looked down to see the direction Gretchen had come from was blocked by a white van. The door was sliding open. It would have had to cross traffic and pull up on the sidewalk to be facing that direction. I glanced the other way and saw a second white fan had plowed into the back of our extraction van and again, the sliding door was opening.

I threw Doc Douchebag against the dumpster and drew my 1911. I didn't think, and then I never really seemed to when it came to moments like that. I felt the pull of the Wrath and I went with it, letting it guide and fuel me. My own killer instinct honed by the power of the Sword.

I got a good grip with both hands on the pistol, I got a good sight picture and sight alignment. I felt my finger on the trigger pressing gently and steadily. The pistol barked in my hand but already I was reacquiring my sight picture as I moved forward.

The sliding door was opening but the front passenger door hung limp as the .45 ACP round pierced through the window and found purchase in the temple of the passenger. Blood and brain splattered on the windshield and the driver.

My second shot rang and the spent shell casing arched through the air. The hollow point bullet passed through the widening aperture of the sliding door. It punched into the man in the gap's plate carrier sending him back against the man behind him. I quickly snapped a third shot catching him in the throat. Blood gushed like a Super Soaker arching water as the arterial bleed let loose.

Behind me, I heard the familiar *rat-tat-tat-tat-tat-tat* of AK-47 fire. Jammer cooked off a nine-round burst, longer than was normally optimal but in the confines of the alley, I was sure that each round found the van if not a person.

Gretchen had her pistols free of their holsters and her cape billowing behind her like a damned superhero. The simple fact of gunfighting is two-gun pistoleers don't tend to hit squat. But Gretchen wasn't cooking rounds in rapid succession out of both guns or firing both pistols at once. Instead, she stood perpendicular to her target with one pistol down and the other up and out. She squeezed off one shot then calmly cocked the single action pistol with her thumb and carefully aimed for the next shot. She wasn't fast, but she was accurate.

Her first shot punched into the van's sliding door as it was opening. The door was opened by the time her second shot let fly. Her round through the door had caught the guy pulling it in the arm. The guy was on his knee as he pulled the door open; her third shot punched in the left side of his knee, passed back into his leg shattering his femur and doing some damage to his hip bone as it exited more or less out of his taint. Her fourth shot punched into his chest above the top of his plate carrier, just to the right of his left strap shattering his collar and shoulder socket.

I sprinted ahead of her but cognizant to stay out of her line of fire. I knew the closer I got to them the more options I had. I felt the rage, I felt the Sword wanting to unsheathe itself and give the world what God knew it deserved. I focused it in the pistol. I had a shot and I took it.

The man in the back of the van that my second target had fallen upon had finally slung his companion off him. To my amazement the guy was carrying a goddamned grenade launcher, an HK-169 40mm single-shot side breach-loading one to be exact. He never got to use it as I shot him in his closed mouth and blew his teeth out the base of the back of his goddamned head.

The fourth guy in the back of the van had a grenade in his hand and had jerked the pin free. It was a shot I never could have made before. It was a shot I couldn't have made now were it not for the rage of the Sword channeled into the pistol, guiding my eye and my grip giving me preternatural aim. The bullet blew off two of his fingers and knocked the grenade out of his hand. It clattered to the floor of the van; the last I saw of the guy was the fear in his eyes under his baklava. Fuck him.

I turned and got between Gretchen and the van and ran back toward her. She lifted her aim and her bent elbow aimed the barrel straight up as I got to her and put my arms around her. The grenade went off in the van behind me and I heard several of the grenadiers 40-mike mikes cook-off as well. I felt the pressure wave but that was the extent for us. It wasn't a huge movie fireball, but a big violent puff of smoke that happened to take out the van.

"Did you fucking see that?" She smiled in amazement as we both turned and started running toward the burning car to help Jammer.

"Yep." I nodded as my Chucks pounded the pavement.

As we got to the car I saw Dr. Douchebag standing, and then I realized it wasn't Dr. Douchebag. He had grown nearly a foot and possessed a musculature that a gym rat would have murdered for. The blonde hair was no longer hair but more like individual bone protrusions from the skull that would bristle-like fur on a mongoose's back. His eyes burned, literally fucking burned. His forearms were sliced from the elbow down to his wrist and blood was everywhere. His fingernails were not four-inch black talons.

Dr. Eric Travis Ph.D. had tried to use his own blood to summon a demon to protect him and got way more than he fucking bargained for.

The Demon smiled as he looked at me.

Situation

Normal

All

Fucked

Up

Well, in light of a goddamned, literally, demon our lot in life had just been upgraded from SNAFU to FUBAR.

Fucked

Up

Beyond

All

Repair

I switched my 1911 to my left hand and unsheathed the Fiery Sword.

Chapter Twenty-One: FUBAR with a Capital F

Whiskey In The Jar by Thin Lizzy

Gretchen pulled to a stop next to me as she saw the Fiery Sword in my hand and the demon before us. She then made the decision that the best tactical option was for her to run around the other side of the still burning car; it was that or she just said *fuck that* and went around. Either way, it left me with a burning blade in my hand, a 1911 in the other, and a demon before me.

According to the stuff Megatron pulled off the Akashic Network, Berith was a demon that you sacrifice a chicken to; you get a deal and it gets your soul. Baalberieth, on the other hand, was the Archdemon of Murder. Judging from the painful-looking ax that was forming in his hands I was guessing this bastard wasn't here to bargain. Out of his back wings were forming; they looked like they were made of coagulated blood and were forming as the blood dripped in directions that would give a physics teacher a heart attack.

"YOU!" it roared in a voice that was both masculine and feminine, as if multiple voice actors were sharing a microphone and reading the exact same lines even if they were slightly off rhythm.

Baalberieth swung the ax. I didn't need the skill of the Sword to know that I wasn't going to parry that swing. So I got out of the damn way, ducking under it, feeling the low pressure of air left behind it as it passed over me before hitting the burning car and sending it three feet in the air to smash into the opposite wall of the alley. Zadkiel had been good, but Baalberieth was definitely stronger. Thank God Gretchen was already past the car and moving toward Jammer, who had emptied his AK magazine and was reloading.

"Disappointing Nephew!" it barked.

I got my footing in time for him to bring the ax back at me in the backswing. It came in low, just at knee level. I jumped and tucked my knees to my chest. The ax looked like it was made from lava that quickly cooled as it came from a vent under the ocean. It was a thick gray and black with lines of molten rock running along it. It smoked like a forty-three-year-old waitress who didn't want to die but did secretly hope emphysema would drop the curtain a little short so she'd never again need to remember the day's specials. I held my breath as it passed under me, and even doing that I felt the sulfur in my eyes. I hacked down with the Fiery Sword and cut an inch-deep gouge from just below his left elbow to just above his left wrist.

The slice didn't seem to bother him at fucking all.

His wild, missing swing caused bricks to explode from the force of the impact as the ax bit into the building. I landed and he charged at me. I barely rolled to the side fast enough and still took a bit of the impact. But I reflexively lashed out with the Sword, letting it do what it wanted. The tip tore along the right calf of the demon, even though at this point the knees bent the wrong goddamn way.

Horns were starting to grow out of his forehead and even though his face still resembled the former Dr. Eric Travis, Doc Douchebag was gone.

He roared. It was the sound of a slaughterhouse. It was the sound of Viking pillage. It was the sound of Pagans being burned to death in the Northern Crusade. It was the sound of men being forced to watch *Steel Magnolias*.

I was almost knocked over by the blast of air as the coagulated wings began to beat. The wings looked unnatural like there were two extra unnecessary joints to the bones. Baalberieth lifted into the air. He glowered at me with his burning, baleful eyes and pointed with the—what I assumed—brimstone ax and began to fly up and away from the alley.

I felt the tug of the Sword. I wanted to chase him. I wanted to punish the archdemon. I wanted to make him feel the displeasure of the Father for his betrayal and disregard of the divine plan. I wanted to rip into him for not being there to save my mother from Zadkiel. I wanted to crush him for no other reason than to fucking crush him. But I couldn't fucking fly, and I could hear gunfire from the other end of the alley.

So I turned and started charging down the alley. Jammer didn't have any real cover so he was using the only protection he had: volume of fire. Gretchen was behind a garbage can that probably wouldn't stop a high-powered pellet gun, but at least it gave her concealment as she reloaded her two pistols with cartridges from her belt.

The alley was blocked, not by our van but by theirs. There were several dead or dying men in the van who had been caught trying to come out of their own van. But the back doors were wide open as well. Men had gotten behind the van and were using it as cover.

I started sprinting. They had the audacity to shoot at the people I cared about. The Fiery Sword flared in my hand and I sprinted at a pace Usain Bolt couldn't have kept up with and I only managed by the Wrath of God. I jumped and kicked. My foot dented in the cab of the van pushing into the ceiling distorting all of it, but it was enough pressure to tip the van on its driver's side wheels and onto its side. I landed on top of it even as I heard the crunch as two or three men were crushed under it.

To my right Switch was up and crumping away with the AA-12 at a second van which had positioned to cut off ours. I saw a third van to my left with another Tac Team of four plus a driver positioned. I leaped to my left and started rushing the van fifty meters away.

The road and sidewalk were basically empty. People had fled their cars or cowered in them. People had darted from the sidewalks into a building or away from the fray. Even if there were a few men of action in the mix, it must have been so confusing they didn't know what side to take, having then decided that doing nothing was better than being wrong. It made our fight cleaner though. My Chuck Taylors slapped the pavement as I ran and vaulted over the hood of a quickly parked and probably even more quickly emptied car.

I emptied my .45 into one unfortunate man, but he was armed with an HK-169 grenade launcher so it's not like he was really a bystander. I forced my 1911 into the waist of my pants and grabbed the Fiery Sword with both hands. The blade grew from nineteen inches to close to thirty-six.

I got to the corpse of the Grenadier in time to see his friend come around the van with a 12-gauge pump. I let go of the Sword with my left hand and the blade shrunk back to nineteen inches. I reached down and grabbed the corpse of the grenadier and lifted him before me like a shield. Two shells worth of buckshot punched into the back of the body I shielded myself with, as I kept moving forward. I got to the back edge of the van and tossed the corpse shield at the shotgunner. I heard the *umph* and the clattering of gear as the man was knocked over.

The Sword told me to duck low as I came around the van. I did, coming around finding myself at almost waist level of a guy with FN automatic rifle aimed over my head. I grabbed the foregrip of the Belgium-made weapon and jerked it down and to the left. The elbow between the barrel and magazine well wedged in my shoulder as I stabbed in and up with the Fiery Sword. The Wrath of God easily tore through the man's ballistic plates and carrier as I gutted him from hip to throat.

In the distance, I could hear the sounds of the fight going on. The chain *snaps* of the AK, the *bumps* of the AA-12, and even the *crump-boom* of a grenade launcher. I wanted to kill them all and send them to their disappointed Father, but at the moment I might as well have been a world away.

I spun on my knee away and to my left so his body would fall past me as I let my right arm with the Sword swing wide, cutting the man behind him off at the knees. He hit the ground hard and wailed, but to his credit, he was trying to get his shotgun into the fight. I half-hopped, half-kipped up from my knees to land with my knees hard on his chest as I pushed the Fiery Sword under his chin and out the top of his skull.

I would have died had the Sword not screamed for me to roll. I rolled to the left and across the pavement as the shotgun blast peppered the side of the van in line with where I just was. I stopped and rolled to my right back toward the corpse as another shotgun blast chipped the concrete where I had just been rolling. I reverse somersaulted to my feet and saw the shotgunner from earlier racking his weapon to get another shell in the chamber. He'd half-pulled himself from under the grenadier's corpse.

I reached down and grabbed the corpse at my feet and flung it. The body caught the shotgun blast in the air but that didn't stop the second body from landing on the shooter. I rushed forward and stabbed down through the corpse into the man underneath. He'd had some fight to him, but not after that.

"Nick!" I heard her scream.

I felt the violence in my mind. I felt the dark wrathful place trying to drag me deeper into the glorious freedom of becoming oblivion. I wanted to punish everyone for their failures in the eyes of the Father. I wanted to burn the goddamned world for not living up to His vision. I wanted to pay humanity the wages of its failure and banality. I wanted every insipid mouth to choke on its own bile. I wanted to burn the fucking world to a goddamned cinder then dance on it.

"NICK!" I heard the voice and I recognized it from someplace even in the animal part of my brain that wanted nothing more than to eat, fight, or fuck. In retrospect maybe it was the raw attraction she held over me that kept saving me. Maybe it was the raw animal instinct, the biological urge to fuck that saved me. Maybe because of it she could reach past the rage and find the other animal me and drag me back to manhood.

I watched the better angel of my nature come around the corner. The cape was gone and she had a belt of twelve 40mm HEDP rounds strung across her chest and one of the HK-169s in her hands. There is a small gap in the breach, which you can use to check if anything is in the chamber. Now whether it was a spent shell or a live round was up for debate, but there was definitely something in there.

I saw the fear in her eyes. It was always there when I was like this. I didn't know if it was fear of me or for me, and I was always too embarrassed to ask.

I let go of my right hand and the Fiery Sword burned itself out of my grasp. "It's me..." I muttered, a little surprised I found my voice.

She smiled weakly with fear in her eyes. "It's always you."

"Yeah," I nodded in agreement, "but it's *me* me."

She grabbed my hand and started pulling me. "It's bad, Nick, we have to go."

I stepped with her, moving into a sprint. "The demon?"

"No, it's worse." I saw she had tears rolling down her cheeks, leaving streaks in the post-gunfight/fire grime on her normally gentle features. Her voice cracked, "It's so much worse."

Chapter Twenty-Two: I Have Lived In An Age Of Heroes

He Ain't Heavy by Neil Diamond

I found myself behind the wheel of one of the ambush vans tearing down Salerno Street haphazardly wearing through traffic with the uncaring deftness of the Fates. Jammer lay in the back with his head propped up on a backpack filled with something or other wearing the bemused approving smile of a proud father showing his son the unmodified versions of *Star Wars* in which Han Solo shoots first. He had his hands over his gut and blood was oozing around his fingers. Switch lay in the floor, passed out and head rolling side to side with the careening of the van through traffic. Gretchen sat on her knees trying to stay balanced as she tore through Jammer's aid bag.

"What am I looking for?" she asked in a voice that was as frantic as my driving.

"Well," Jammer said calmly, "that wad of stuff in your hand, toss that to me."

Gretchen tossed the small package to Jammer without even looking. He caught it with a bloody hand and tore it open with his teeth before pushing it to the wound in his gut.

"Okay, Gretchen, I don't want to freak you out," Jammer said calmly. "I don't want to freak you out, but Switch is totally fucked if you don't save him. But I'm here to talk you through it. So it's gonna be groovy. Say that with me, okay? Groovy."

I glanced back in the mirror and saw Gretchen's eyes wide, frantic. "Groovy."

I saw Jammer give his overly physical wink. "Groovy, doll, now first grab a bottle of water and some gauze."

"What about gloves?" she asked with a shaking voice.

Jammer chuckled. "You're already wearing them, doll."

"Oh." She dug through the pack and grabbed some gauze, ripping open the package with her teeth. "Now what?"

"Grab the scissors and slice his pants crotch to knee. We got to see what we're working with." Jammer spoke calmly, like a professional deep in his craft; the definition of the Chuck Yeager Deadpan-Danger voice.

I heard the cut and then a rip of fabric. I whipped the van around a pizza delivery car and almost clipping a bike messenger. I kept my foot to the floor, the RPMs running almost into the red as I pushed the motor as hard as I could.

"Okay," Jammer told her, "bend his knee toward his gut, that's gonna relieve the tension of the skin of his pelvis." She must have been doing what Jammer told her because he kept going on. "Now take two fingers and push it between his junk and his leg to get his pulse."

I knocked over a garbage can when I hopped the curve with the passenger side tires.

"Okay, I got the pulse," Gretchen screamed with satisfaction.

"Good girl, now pinch the skin right over the pulse."

"Okay, got it," she assured him.

"Okay, stripper, take a scalpel from the surgical kit and slice that pinch of skin. Now cut that fucker and do it deep. Deep. Don't worry, you're pinching that skin so you don't fuck up arteries, nerves, and tendons and shit."

"Oh, God..." Gretchen groaned.

"He's not here, Gretchen, this is just you and me," Jammer assured her in the most unassuming way. "You're doing fine. Not as good as me but great for a stripper." You could hear the smile in his voice. "Good, now let go of the pinch and start dabbing with the gauze. Okay, lemme see?" I heard Jammer sigh. "Sorry, stripper, but rookie move: you didn't make the hole big enough."

"Sorry..." You could hear the tears in Gretchen's voice.

"Just get the slit bigger and keep dabbing with the gauze." Jammer was calm, reassuring, and absolutely professional. "Okay, find the pulse again."

It was quiet for a second and I lost what was being said as the tires screeched in a turn.

"Nick," Jammer said calmly. "If you kill us before we get to University Hospital all this work your girlfriend is doing is gonna get pissed away."

"Doing my best, Jammer..."

"I know, buddy." I saw him smile in the mirror.

"Okay, Gretchen, find the pulse again." She must have nodded. "Okay, grab the curved Kellys out of the bag with your right hand. Now push those fuckers closed, tip down onto the pulse. When you got it, open the tips and tear away any fat or shit in the way to get on top of that fucking artery."

"Artery?" Gretchen asked, the seriousness of the wound landing on her.

"Yeah," Jammer confirmed, "I'm pretty sure Switch's femoral artery has been totally transacted."

"Oh, God..." Gretchen gasped.

"Yeah, his femur's fractured too but that's for later. It's the artery that's gonna kill him if you don't get your shit together, Gretchen." Jammer wasn't flustered or hurried, even though all of us knew a cut artery was a recipe for fucked cake. "Now rip shit with those curved Kellys you got to expose that artery."

I heard Gretchen cry, but I also heard Gretchen working. "Okay, okay, I think I got it."

"Okay, good girl. Now clamp the artery with the curved Kellys. And clamp that shit as far away from the heart as you can. Now those things click when you close them. Don't go more than three clicks, okay?"

"Why three?" Gretchen asked.

"More than three will fuck up the artery." Jammer instructed with a professor like calm. "Now, there's some suture in the aid bag, grab it and tie a stupid tight fisherman's knot below the clamp. Do that twice."

I took the mirror off an F-150 but now I could see the entrance to the emergency room of University Hospital.

"Okay, you got those knots?" Jammer asked.

"Yes," Gretchen assured him.

"Good, now unclick the curved Kellys down to one click, okay?"

"Okay..." Gretchen said tightly.

"Well, bad news," Jammer sighed.

"What?" Gretchen screamed.

"You saved his life. Now you're gonna have to put up with that son of a bitch. When we pull up at the hospital, Gretchen, you push him out and, Nick, you drive the fuck off."

I tore up the drive and hopped the curve in between an ambulance. I looked back and Gretchen pulled open the sliding door and hopped out. She grabbed Switch by his shoulders and hauled him out onto the sidewalk, while screaming, "Help!"

The second Switch was out Jammer yelled, "Get in here, stripper! Nick, get us out of here!"

I checked in the mirror and saw Gretchen dive in as I floored it. Gretchen grabbed the back of the passenger seat and pull the door shut. She turned and knelt next to Jammer. "Okay, what do I do for you? Why didn't we drop you off at the hospital?"

Jammer reached up and patted Gretchen's cheek. "You don't do nothing, doll, and we didn't drop me up because I'm fucking dead."

My eyes darted to him in the mirror. He met my eyes in the mirror. "It's good, Nick." He smiled. "It's all good."

"Jammer, there's gotta be a way..." Gretchen was crying.

Jammer gave the gauze in his hands a squeeze. "This fucker's stuck in my spine, and on top of that, I'm pretty sure it's punctured my aorta. I had ten minutes when I got hit. Now, I'm probably gonna be awake for another three or four minutes."

"Jammer." Gretchen wept. "Tell me what to do!"

He smiled. "Will you lay my head in your lap. If I can't go out seeing something glorious I want to go out seeing something pretty."

I almost drove into a telephone pole. I had to force my eyes back on the road. "Jammer."

"It's okay, Nick," he assured me.

"You sure?" I asked tearing around a corner trying to get us back to the warehouse.

"Yeah, I can't feel anything under my nipples, and I'm bleeding out. This is happening."

"Goddammit, Jammer."

"It's cool, Nick. We all go out." I looked in the mirror and saw him smile. "I got to go out saving Switch. What's better than that?"

"Jesus, Jammer, this is my fault," I muttered.

He laughed weakly. "Goddamn right it is... if you'd not been such a likable cockbag I'd just be a disillusioned maker of mescaline and grower of pot. Fuck you for making my life interesting."

"Jammer..."

"Tell Switch we're square." Jammer's voice was already getting light and airy.

I've been in some crazy situations where at the time I knew I was going to die and ended up being wrong. But this, Jammer, like this.

I felt my fist bang the steering wheel. "Goddammit," I muttered. I hit it again and again and again. "Goddammit goddammit goddammit GOD-FUCKING-DAMNIT!!!!"

"Nick!" Gretchen screamed over me.

I looked back to her in the mirror, the anguish on her face. She wept, but Jammer smiled. Just smiled. There was a cherubic look to his bearded face. Jammer was the most energetic person I'd ever know. He was a world of motion. But now, lying there with his head in Gretchen's lap he looked peaceful, calm. It was natural looking and unnatural looking all at the same time.

He nodded; he knew.

I tore down the street and into the warehouse screeching to a stop. I tore open the door and started running around the van.

"What happened?" Megatron asked, but I ignored her.

I opened the sliding door and saw Jammer smiling up to Gretchen. She stroked his bearded face with her lithe fingers. I reached out and he reached up squeezing my hand. I held tight, like the harder I could squeeze the longer I could keep him here.

"Nick," Jammer gasped, his voice was getting light, his breathing shallow. His dark eyes met mine. "Tell Switch he doesn't owe me."

"I will."

"Tell Chris,"—Chris was Jammer's brother—"Tell Chris that I make better marinara than he does."

I couldn't help but smile. "I will."

"Gretchen." Jammer looked up to her. "You gotta take care of Nick. I'm... fuck, this sucks. I'm fucked, I'm not gonna be here to take care of him. Fuck knows he needs it."

Gretchen's tears rained down onto Jammer's forehead. He didn't seem to mind.

"If I can't see something glorious," Jammer gasped, "at least I can see something pretty."

I heard Megatron weeping behind me; she'd obviously put together what was happening.

I felt the pull of the Sword. I felt the rage. I wanted to make the world pay for me losing my best friend. The Father wanted his due. I wanted to behead every fucking Teutonic Knight on the planet. I wanted to burn their safe houses and strongholds.

Gretchen wept. Megatron cried. Switch was at a hospital and who knew if what Gretchen and Jammer had done in the back of the van would work. I felt my best friend's hand getting weaker in my grasp.

I felt the tug of the Sword and I didn't want to fight it. Maybe that's how addiction worked, the willingly subsuming yourself into a temporary good feeling. Letting something else help you forget. I could have burned the world and not felt the impotence of the moment.

My best friend was dying and there was fuck all I could do about it.

"If I can't see something glorious, at least I can see something pretty," Jammer had said.

I knew it was our last moments.

"Jammer," I asked solemnly, "where's the Pig Gun?"

He smiled, blood oozing from his lips and he pointed to a tough box. I opened it and pulled the M-60 Echo free. I popped the feed tray and loaded the rounds from the sack magazine clipped underneath. I slammed the feed tray shut and yanked back on the charging handle. I didn't thumb on the safety. I wouldn't need it.

I looked to Jammer and nodded. "Smoke me a kipper, I'll be back for breakfast."

He wept, but smiled and whispered, "See you, Space Cowboy."

And then, without inhaling again, the world lost a hero. Jammer was my guy for that.

Chapter Twenty-Three: Simple Economics

Fire and Rain by James Taylor

I felt numb, and I hated myself for it.

I wanted to feel grief. I wanted to feel rage. I wanted to feel the Fiery Sword try and drag me into the blissful oblivion of violent delight. I wanted to feel anything but nothing; because anything would have made me feel real. Feeling anything would have been human.

Gretchen cried and held his head in her lap. She stroked his hair and beard gently. Like Lenny always wanted to with the rabbits but always failed at; yet she succeeded, not that it mattered. Her face was red and blotchy as she wept. She looked like I imagined Mary to look when her son was taken off the cross, the way Eve looked when she found Abel, the way Sarah looked when her husband and son went for a walk up the mountain. Unlike Christ, he wasn't waking up in three days to open his coffin and say, "What'd I miss?" Unlike Isaac, Zadkiel wasn't going to show up to stay his would-be killer's hand. He couldn't even if he'd wanted; I'd already killed the archangel. Eve was the only one really applicable. Gretchen was every girl that lost a friend in a righteous fight.

Gretchen cried and held his head in her lap. Gretchen cried and I envied her that.

We'd always said life was simple economics. The reason life was valuable was that it was finite. It ended, thus creating the scarcity. Scarcity of a needed or wanted commodity upped its value. To a kid on a beach, sand had no value. To a guy on top of Everest, a bottle of O2 could be worth its weight in gold. Life ended, irrevocably, thus what life you had was the most precious thing in the world. Jammer and I had always agreed on that.

But life had a value beyond your own self. Jammer's life had mattered, and always would, to me and to her. Now he was gone.

I knew it wasn't my fault and I knew it was. I knew I'd always wonder what I could have and should have done and I knew I'd know I couldn't have done any better. I knew I'd understand and I knew I wouldn't. I knew he was dead, and I knew anything else to consider was just mental masturbation.

I don't know how long I stood there. I don't know how long she sat there stroking his face. I don't guess it would ever matter to Jammer.

The silence was finally broken as I whispered, "Where are they?" Some people would have asked the same question to mean *do you know where they are*, but I knew she knew. "You don't have to come, I know you've had qualms, and I understand. I do." I could hear the pleading in my voice. The nothing I felt being replaced by a need in my gut. "But I need to know."

She gently, lovingly lifted his head off her lap and laid it on the floor of the warehouse. She stood and walked over to a worktable and started taking .357 shells from a box and loading them into the empty loops of her pistol belt.

I walked over to Megatron, who stood by her laptop with her hands over her mouth as her eyes wept for Jammer in a way I knew no one would cry for me. I held the M-60 in one hand and the belt clattered as I lowered the barrel to the floor, holding the medium machine-gun it in my right hand. I put my left hand on Megatron's shoulder and gave it a squeeze.

"Megatron." She didn't look at me as I spoke. I gave her a gentle shake. "Grand Vizier Megatron Terabyte the Cyber Samurai. I need you."

Her eyes met mine even through the wall of tears barely contained in them.

"Pack up and go to the hospital. Switch is there. I don't care what you do—hack your way in or what—but get there, be there when he wakes up."

She glanced to Jammer.

I reached up and turned her chin to look at me. "Switch is gonna wake up. Jammer saw to that, okay?" She nodded and I continued. "So what are you going to do?"

"I'm..." she lost her voice but swallowed and found it. "I'm going to the hospital for Switch."

I managed to smile. "Good girl. It's up to you now, go get it done."

She nodded bravely and packed up her laptop and tablet. She put her bag in a car Jammer had left in the warehouse then walked over to Gretchen who silently was reloading one of her revolvers since her cartridge belt was restocked. Megatron didn't stop her or say anything. She simply wrapped her arms around Gretchen from behind and rested her head on her shoulder. The blonde hair meeting the raven waves like different colored sands in an artistic design. I heard Megatron sniff and saw Gretchen reach back across her body to gently pat Megatron's cheek.

Megatron didn't look to me at all as she got in the car and drive away. I didn't know if I was ever going to see her again; whether from her simply driving away and never coming back or from me getting killed. It didn't really seem to matter either way.

I carried the M-60 over to the van and set it next to the driver's seat. I walked back to the tough box and started pulling out green metal boxes of 7.62 NATO linked cartridges with one tracer in every five-round mix. I pulled the lids off the boxes and started pulling out the cloth sacks containing the waxed cardboard boxes each containing a hundred-round breakaway belt. I pulled the belts out of the boxes and lay them on the worktable, getting both belts from each green ammo can before reaching for the next.

In the tough box, Jammer had had five soft "magazines," each holding one hundred rounds. In the military, we'd affectionately referred to these as "Nut Sacks." One of these I'd already attached to the M-60, so there were four Nut Sacks left.

I had five hundred rounds in Nut Sacks and two thousand rounds lying on the table. I heard Gretchen behind me watching. She was done reloading her pistols.

"Can you get me a backpack?" I asked without looking as I started attaching my hundred-round belts together. By the time I was finished making a two thousand-round belt—an "Infini-Belt" as I used to refer to it when I was humping an M-249 SAW in Fallujah—she had brought me a North Face backpack from the van. I slowly added the belted ammo letting the rounds go back and forth over each other like an accordion. A hundred rounds of belted 7.62 weighed seven-point-one pounds. So the backpack ended up weighing more than a hundred-and-forty-two pounds.

I felt the anger, I felt the rage, and I felt the Sword. I knew the stupid thing. I wanted to do. God, it would have felt great. I grabbed the bag and hurled it twenty-five feet into the van making it rock on its shocks. "GODDAMNIT!!!" I could feel her eyes on me. I grabbed the table and flipped it. I seethed, and I knew what I had to do.

"I need you to make a call." My voice was quiet, but there was nothing but iron behind it.

"Who?" she asked; her voice was equally quiet, but there was no timidity to it.

"Whoever is in charge," I said slowly and deliberately as I looked to her. There was confusion in her eyes and will. Always, there was will. "I need a meet."

"Nick," she said my name slowly, buying time to try and work out my angle. "Why?"

"I know what I'm doing," I half-growled. I fought the rage, I wanted a blood bath, but I wanted to win, for Jammer. "We killed them all, right?"

She nodded.

"Then they don't know we don't have Doc Douchebag." I felt my lips turn up at the corners. "They wanted him for a reason. So in the short run, we got an advantage because they might not know about the goddamned demon that got unleashed."

She softly smiled. It was bold and she knew it. But in a choice between bold and suicidal or... She took a phone out of one of her pouches. Our eyes never separated as she held the phone to her ear. I didn't hear a voice on the other end, but I heard Gretchen start speaking. "We got what you want. We want a meet."

"Tell them their turf," I said quietly.

Her eyes were wide; there was fear there, but she didn't waver. "Your place. I know where it is." She hung up the phone and smashed it under her heel.

"You don't have to go," I said quietly. I couldn't meet her eyes. Jammer had been right; I didn't blame her. I couldn't meet her eyes because I didn't want her to feel like I was really asking her to go. I didn't want to meet her eyes and see something in mine that made her feel like I needed her to go. I did. I was about to commit suicide and I knew it. If committing suicide is killing yourself than any guy who died pushing a kid out of the way from getting hit by a bus, every guy who jumped on a grenade for his friends, everyone who willing chose to die when they had a way out was a suicide. But there's an inherent nobility to that and selfishness to the other.

I was about to go and get myself killed because Jammer's death demanded action and if my death was the price of it then so fucking be it.

"I do," she answered as she sat on the ground next to a spilled box of double-ought buckshot and started loading shotgun shells into the drums for the AA-12.

"I'm sorry." I didn't know what else to say, but I knew I couldn't say anything.

"They are the only family I've ever known." Her voice never wavered even as the tears silently traveled down her cheeks.

I stopped and turned to face her. I wrapped my arms around her and pulled her to me, causing her to drop a shell and the drum. She cried into my shirt. I took her face in my hands and made her look into my eyes. "You wouldn't be doing this right now if that were true."

"Nick..."

"People don't go to the mattresses for friends, you don't put it all on the line for people who don't matter."

"Nick..." she wept.

"We're your fucking family, Gretchen."

She wrapped her arms around my neck and pulled her face into my shoulder and sobbed.

"When Jammer and I came for you, we did it because you are fucking family." I held the back of her head and felt her breath warm my collar. "There are two types of family, the one we're given and the one we find." I turned my head and spoke into her hair. "And I know which one is worth more. And Jammer knew which one was worth dying for."

She kissed me. It was a kiss of pain, the kiss of a person trying to bury their pain in something that comforted them. It was the kiss of a post-funeral-desperate-to-feel-alive fuck. But that didn't mean there wasn't love behind it. Our lips lingered before parting with glacial speed.

"I love you," she whispered, as if she said it louder would make it less real.

I smiled softly. "I know."

She blushed and a smile touched her lips. "Han Solo, really?"

I shrugged because I didn't really have an answer better than that.

She slowly turned out of my arms and let go of my neck as we got back to work.

We finished reloading the drums for the AA-12. I finished packing the Infini-Belt and loaded it in the van with the other Nut Sacks. I then opened the breach of the HK-169. It opened to the side and I pulled out the round; it was an HEDP: High Explosive Dual Purpose.

I thought about the inventory. Thirteen HEDP rounds for an HK-169, two thousand five hundred rounds of 7.62 link for an M-60, five twenty-round drums for the AA-12. We might as well go and knock over a Vegas casino.

After loading the van I stopped and undid my belt. I unlooped it until half the belt was undone. I walked over to Jammer and knelt down next to him. I reached up and shut his eyes before I started undoing his belt and pulling off his leather holster and his nickel-plated 1911 with antique ivory grips; his Drug Dealer gun. I fed it onto my belt until it sat in the small of my back under my suit jacket. I got my belt back in place and drew Jammer's pistol, pressure checking the slide to make sure a round was chambered before putting it back.

I didn't kneel again but simply bent over and unfastened his ankle holster with his back up .357 Magnum. I walked over to Gretchen, who wiped her eyes as I held the ankle rig out to her. "We finish this today."

She knelt and buckled it around her jungle boot and made sure it as secure. She looked up to me. "One way or another we're never going to have to bother with them ever again, Nick."

I kissed her.

We loaded into the van and got on the road. She told me where to go and started giving me a description of the layout.

As I drove I took my phone and dialed number three on my speed dial. Number one on the phone was Gretchen, and number three had been Jammer. I heard the phone go straight to voicemail. There wasn't a message, just a beep. I hung up and put my phone back in my pocket.

"Who did you call?" she asked with a downy curiosity.

"Lucifer."

"Voicemail?" There was a little regret in her voice as she asked.

I nodded. He spent a third of his time in heaven, a third of his time in hell, and a third of his time here. Voicemail was inevitable, I guess.

I drove in silence then I decided to pull my phone back out and started playing a song on repeat. We listened to it once, and as it started repeating she said, "This isn't on the Gun Fight Mix."

My eyes met hers. "It is today. It's Jammer's favorite."

She nodded understandingly.

Life was precious because it ends. People are precious because you can't keep them forever. It was simple economics.

"I love you," I told her.

She replied quietly and adamantly, "Han Solo."

Chapter Twenty Four: In Terms Of Silence

The Sound of Silence by Disturbed

Had I had time I would have made some calls. I'd have called Yuri and gotten him to sit up with the Dragunov to provide at a minimum some overwatch and word of what would be going on outside. I'd have called Christian—an ironic phone call for the Devil's nephew to make—for some backup. I'd never worked with Chris; he'd been a leg and Jammer and I had been Airborne, but he was Jammer's brother and unlike mine, he was worth a damn. He'd deserve a chance for some payback. I'd have waited for Switch to get out of the hospital, if he ever did. In honesty, I would have called in a lot of people. But there wasn't time.

They had numbers but we had audacity. They had home-field advantage but we had audacity. They had supplies but we had audacity. They had funding but we had audacity. With six hours and a scale map of the building Gretchen could probably have provided I could have cooked up a five-course meal.

We sat in the van as the radio played.

"Why did he have the sex toys taped to the windows of his loft?" Gretchen asked out of nowhere.

"Huh?"

"Jammer had all those sex toys taped to the windows of his loft." The mix of wonder and curiosity in her voice almost held back the grief. "What was that about?"

I remembered what she was talking about and I couldn't help but laugh. "Well, he was a paranoid son of a bitch."

"Well, he was a drug dealer."

"Drug-producing trafficker," I corrected her.

She smiled softly. "My apologies."

"Well, like I said, he was paranoid. So all those dildos and butt plugs and panty vibrators and such were all set to a remote. He could turn them on and it would fuck up any laser microphone aimed at his windows."

She laughed. "Seriously?"

"No shit." I shrugged. "That's what he told me the reasoning was anyway, and the theory is sound."

She laughed and then we slowly fell into a comforting silence as the song started over.

"Do you remember what you told me after karaoke that first time?" she asked quietly. You could hear the tears in her eyes through her voice.

"You mean Asian karaoke?" I smirked. Thinking of Jammer I just couldn't help it.

She laughed. "Yeah."

I looked to her. She was the most beautiful thing I'd ever seen. She was my world. "Yeah, I remember, and I meant it and I still fuckin' mean it."

"Do we have a plan?" she asked as she found the iron in her voice.

"I was gonna start by fucking any window I can find with 40mm, saving the last two to breach the front door. While I'm doing that you pick whatever you can with the AK. Then ditch it when we start moving in lieu of the AA-12. Let me take point and do the heavy liftin', you pick off stragglers, cover our six, and lay down some fire when I have to change out the belts."

She nodded with a stoic resolve.

"But then I came up with a better one." I don't know if my light tone was reassuring or not, but it was meant to be.

I knew I should have brought the spare barrel for the M-60, but with three thousand rounds, at the rate we were probably going to go, I wasn't going to take the time to change the barrels. The machine gun was going to be slag by the time I was done with it and I couldn't find a fuck to give about it.

"If we go in the front way it'll be a trap," she told me as the song started over again.

"I know," I assured her. "We're not playing it straight."

I glanced to the target building as we drove past the drive up to it. It was one of those crazy large Southern Baptist Mega Churches. Apparently, the Teutonic Knights, or whatever they'd become in the modern times, like housing in churches. "How do you know about this place?"

She chewed her lip for a moment then met my eyes. "It's my mother's headquarters."

It didn't take very long for that to sink in. "Your mom's in there?"

She nodded. "Probably. She's who I called."

"Gretchen..." I started but she cut me off softly as she reached over and took my hand.

"Let's finish this, Nick." Her soft hand squeezed my rough fingers. "For Jammer."

We left the van running as the music played. There was no point in turning the van off; we'd never come back to it. In all honesty, we were probably never coming back to anything. We'd probably see Jammer before we ever saw Switch or Megatron or Joy with an E-Y again.

I pulled on one of the plate carriers we'd gotten from the Tac Team at Megatron's. I'd stripped off all the pouches since I wasn't carrying the same load-out as them, making those pouches useless except for the flashbang pouches. I had six flashbangs on my chest rack. Gretchen didn't take a plate carrier. In all honesty with her size a round hitting the plates would probably knock her out of the fight anyway. At least that's what I told myself. Her job today was stealth trooper and backup. I was our Storm Trooper, in the World War 1 sense, not the useless *Star Wars* paradigm.

I saw Gretchen attach four flash bangs to her pouch belt and hook two in the tops of her boots.

"Remember, if you're tossing a banger call 'flash out.' Got it?" I told her with a strange sense of calm considering what was about to go down.

"Good to know." She smiled reassuringly. She might have already known to do that. Maybe she was just letting me feel important.

I pulled the belt of twelve HEDP rounds across my chest like a bandoleer and then pulled the single-point sling over my neck and left arm so the HK-169 dangled down. Then I took a piece of duct tape and strapped it to my left thigh so it wouldn't bounce around as we would try and sneak as close as we could. I lifted the M-60E6 and closed the bipod legs. I didn't hold the machine gun by the gangster grip attached to the foregrip, but instead, I held it like a rifle and just used the gangster grip so the edge of my palm could apply pressure back into my shoulder. I extended the buttstock and brought it to my shoulder. It was the first time I'd carried a belt fed at a professional "low ready" since I was in Fallujah—or was it Afghanistan? I couldn't remember. I had a satchel with four Nut Sacks in it, but I left the Infini-Belt in the van.

Gretchen stepped close and lightly kissed me. It was more that her lips brushed lightly over mine. It was the pressure and feel of a butterfly kiss, but somehow more.

She led the way, AK in her hands and the AA-12 tight across her back. We left the parking lot and crossed into a wood line that created the back of the super church's property. I'd always been quiet back in the military, but Gretchen was something to behold. That said even if you beheld it you probably wouldn't have noticed she was there. If I moved like a breeze through the trees she was the stillness of the grave in terms of noise.

I spotted the guy around the same time she did. She slowly sunk to her knee and set the AK aside and laid the AA-12 with it. I took a knee and brought the M-60 to my shoulder and drew a bead on the guy as Gretchen disappeared into the bush. He was dressed in business casual attire, khakis and a sick pink polo shirt that probably had a fancy color name. Everything was innocuous about the guy except for the Motorola radio with throat mic and earbud and the HK MP7 held lazily in one hand with a single-point sling up over his right shoulder.

It was almost like he was carrying the submachine gun like a purse.

I saw the arc of blood explode from his throat. The razor-like shuriken had sliced through his left jugular. It was so sharp he didn't feel it. He was as surprised as I was to see the blood gush. Before he could even make a sound Gretchen was on his back with her knee and momentum driving him to the ground even as she latched her hand over his mouth. Her free hand pushes two knuckles into his throat, pinching his still intact right jugular. He didn't die as fast as he probably would have wanted, but he died quietly.

She didn't even look for the shuriken. She simply took a large rock and smashed his skull in, for "just in case" reasons, I guess. She silently made her way back to me and handed me the radio and earbud.

I clipped the radio on my belt and pushed the mic and earbud up behind my shoulder and out the collar of my jacket before sticking the bud in my left ear. I moved to the corpse and grabbed his submachine gun and went to a crook of a tree. I set it there with one of the Nut Sacks from the satchel.

We continued on our way as quietly as I could. Gretchen was still far quieter. She could have gone as unnoticed as a fart in a sewer were it not for me.

We came across another innocuously dressed guard with a very nocuous submachine gun. Gretchen again stowed her weaponry and disappeared. She appeared behind the man and got a loop of piano wire over his head and jerked tight around his neck before he could scream. Gretchen jumped up and planted both feet in the small of the man's back, letting gravity pull the piano wire tighter. That guy's pink polo shirt was ruined as he bled like a broken bag of blood. With her weight pulling the piano wire her body was almost perpendicular to the man before he fell. She damn near cut his head off with that piano wire.

This time she returned empty-handed.

"No radio?" I breathed.

Shook her head. "I ruined the cord."

I nodded, understanding as I realized how she'd taken the man out and that the chord for the throat mic and earbud ran up his neck. I went to the second corpse and did the same thing, grabbing his submachine gun and putting it over a branch with another Nut Sack from the satchel.

A little while later we came across a third innocuous guard, but he surprised us as much as we surprised him. He was standing literally with his dick in his hand taking a leak. Before he could scream a shuriken buried itself in his throat opening it like a mouth at his Adam's apple.

Gretchen ran and swung the AK by the barrel like it was a baseball bat and opened a bloody gash along the man's temple. He went down, piss arching as he fell. Gretchen grabbed the AK by the foregrip and the buttstock and started smashing the man's previously handsome features in with the stock.

The good news was she had a radio and earbud now. I walked over to her and gently jogged her arm before leaning in and breathing. "Go get the last guy's radio, we don't need the mic."

She left me with the AK and AA-12. I moved everything a bit away from the newest corpse. I went back and got his submachine gun and stuffed it in a knot in the tree along with another Nut Sack. I kicked about in the dirt until I found a rock that would do. I picked it up and weighed it in my hand as Gretchen miraculously appeared next to me with the radio sans earbud.

"What are you thinking?" Speaking in bare breath wasn't something we had planned, but Gretchen and I had just run with it as a standard in our sneak-sneak. The longer we could sneak-sneak the better.

I took the radio and showed her the rock. I sat the rock against the COM button for speaking. Then I motioned as if I were taping it in place. "These radios aren't party lines. Only one person can talk at a time. So I'm guessing these three are on a security net. When we go loud we can jam that net by taping the rock in place to hot-mic it."

Her eyes shined, still like crime stains under a black light. "That's genius."

"Thanks." I knew I blushed a bit. "There are only sixteen stations on these radios so when we figure out what the backup is we can do the same." I made a spinning motion with my fingers. "Et cetera, et cetera, blah blah blah."

She nodded. "I could see the edge of the wood line up ahead. After that, there are a hundred and fifty meters of parking lot and then the back entrance or loading dock for the kitchens."

She put the AA-12 back over her shoulder and chest down to brush a leaf from the aperture of the second mag. She had two magazines taped together so all she'd have to do is flip them for a quick reload. She didn't have a third. After that, it was going to be AA-12 work—if we made it that far anyway.

I stashed the last Nut Sack behind a tree and took the AA-12 and spare drums from her and stored it behind the same tree. Then I pulled off the HK-169 and the bandolier of HEDP rounds with it.

She checked her grip on the AK. "So we're going in like this?" She managed to smile mischievously and it was goddamned endearing.

"After you." I smiled, hefting the belt fed. "Let's go to motherfuckin' church."

Chapter Twenty-Five: My Big Ass Gambit That I Probably Should Have Briefed Everyone Involved On

The Gambler by Kenny Rogers

We started walking across the parking lot knowing we were probably already being watched. "When it goes to shit we fall back across the parking lot. You know where I stashed everything on the way back?"

"Yes." She raised a quizzical eyebrow. "When it goes to shit?"

"When doesn't it?"

She laughed. That was heartening.

I wished we were fighting the demon or an angel. There is something better about fighting something otherworldly than people. I could enjoy the fight; I could let go to the Sword and revel in the freedom without any consequences. The killing didn't bother me, never had. But fighting a demon or angel felt cleaner. Maybe it's because they didn't leave a corpse to trip on?

"You could go back to the van," I whispered.

She was on my left side. She took the AK and carried it in her left hand. I carried the M-60 in my right with the barrel on my shoulder. She took my hand. Our fingers interlaced.

I squeezed her fingers. "Your Ma gonna like this?"

She laughed out loud and it was hearty. "Not at all."

Four guys in Tac Gear came out of the rear entrance. The four guys didn't matter as much as the two 12-gauges and the two HK MP-7s they were packing.

I put on a smile. "Hey, shitbirds... we have an appointment with your boss."

Gretchen smiled sweetly. "You can check the book, we have an appointment."

The obvious lead guy with the Tac Team gave it away by pushing his finger to his ear digging the earbud deeper in his ear canal like it would get him smarter if he made it reach his brain. I heard the voice in the earbud; it was soft and feminine. "Let them in."

I glanced to Gretchen and she nodded. That told me everything I needed to know.

Hand in hand we approached the door. I tossed the M-60 to one of the goons causing him to drop his shotgun as he struggled to catch the thirtyish pounds of weapon and ammo. Gretchen tossed the AK at another a little harder than was necessary.

The lead goon made to move toward us and motion to one of the others. "Search them."

Gretchen and I looked at each other and then down at the pistols obvious on her hips and the revolver on her boot. Our eyes met and we laughed. I shoved the head goon out of our way and the other stepped quickly to not get the same treatment.

"I'm sure you fine Knights of What Not and Chronic Masturbation got enough weapons to deal with whatever gats we're packing."

"Gats?" I heard the lead goon "You a rapper or something?"

Gretchen laughed and looked demurely over her shoulder. "Actually it came as slang for a Gatling gun but really got popular during the Probation era." I smiled at her and she smiled up at me. "The Continental Op used it as gun slang in *Red Harvest*."

My eyes met hers. "The Dame Derkins." She was my soulmate.

Her smile was a memory to hang on to. "Tracer Bullet." I was the asshole she settled for.

We walked down the hallway past doors that lead to Sunday school rooms and offices. I tried counting the guys I saw but stopped after twenty-five because beyond a quarter a hundred what did it matter?

We came to a large set of double doors and I gestured as I looked behind me. "In there, I take it?"

The goons posted up on the door and Gretchen and I entered. We found ourselves in the back of the Sanctuary to the left of the stage. There were nine of them in total. All female. They each were wearing red gi with black belts, which convinced me they were all probably black belts. On the altar at the front was a five-foot shaft of wood—it looked like ash—and on the tip was a spear point which appeared to be black iron except for the edges, which held slightly discolored waves as you would see on the edge of a katana. The spear tip was a good twelve inches long.

"Hello, mother," Gretchen said coldly; her voice carried in the massive auditorium.

"Daughter." The eldest and central of the figures spoke with an icy voice. A blind man could see the resemblance between the mother and the daughter with the daughter winning in the looks department due to a lack of severity of features.

"What do you want Doc Douchebag for?" I asked. I didn't want to go through a whole he said/she said getting-to-know-you bullshit. We weren't coming out of this as friends, so what was the point in pleasantries?

"Mr. Decker," Gretchen's mother began.

I couldn't help but interrupt her. "Call me Nick." I threw on my most charming smile, which I figured would annoy the living shit out of her.

She chewed the inside of her cheek for a moment. "Nick, Dr. Travis is in possession of knowledge we require."

"Ohhh," I said and whistled like a bomb falling. "'Require' is a pretty big word."

"I take it you did not bring him with you."

I smiled. "Well, if that's how you'll take it that's how I'll give it to you, sister." I gestured to the Spear. "I take it you want Doc McDouche for something about the Spear? Can I help?" I pointed to the tip. "That end goes in the other dude."

I was actually concerned that the Spear was here. I thought they'd be after Doc Douchebag because he had the Spear, but if it was already in their possession what was he needed for?

Gretchen's mother smiled. "Shall I monologue, would that please you, Nick?" The way she said my name was like she was spitting simultaneously.

"In all honesty, it would probably bore me to suicide. No, I'm here because I'm turning myself in."

Her eyebrows arched at that one. That's where Gretchen got it from I guess. "What?"

I looked to Gretchen and hoped—prayed—that she could see where I was going. That she knew I had a plan and wouldn't fuck it up by doing something loving and stupid like I would in her shoes. I looked back to Gretchen's mom. "Me and mine are tired of your bullshit. I..." I paused, Jammer flashed through my mind. "Gretchen walks out of here and goes to tell my crew that it's done. You and yours leave them alone, forever. That's what I get."

"And what do I get?" her mother asked. I felt Gretchen squeezing my hand hard.

I bore my eyes into that bitch like a goddamned laser beam. "I play the Christ card and you get the Fiery Sword."

She stared at me as if she were studying me for an art project. "Where is Dr. Travis?"

"Dead." That was mostly true, and I didn't think they needed to know the fucking details.

Her dark eyes bore into me like she was trying to find oil. "Take him."

I let go of Gretchen's hand and stepped away. I looked to her and found her eyes as assuredly as the sun rises in the east and it being five o'clock somewhere.

It looked like she was about to cry again—it was a day for that—but she held it in. She might not have known what I was doing, but she was backing the play. Maybe she even believed what I had told her mom. Maybe she thought I was doing this to save her. "Han Solo."

She smiled and wiped her left eye with her thumb. "Han Solo." Gretchen reached into my pocket and took my phone. Then she turned and walked slowly back up the row of pews and I started heading toward the altar.

"Take him," her mother commanded, and the other eight women spread out and began approaching me. Two came close and pulled the plate carrier with the flashbangs from my body dropping it in the aisle. Then they pulled the two 1911s from my holsters and threw them together up on the stage.

I had thought I'd come along willingly, but apparently, that didn't mean anything in terms of getting my ass kicked.

Jammer and I had tested the strength the Fiery Sword gave me, and what it boiled down to was I could take five solid shots to the face before it started bothering me. The Sisters in Shadow danced in and out. I took a palm heel to my cheek, a knee to the gut, a heel to the ribs, a knife-hand chop to the back of my neck, a roundhouse kick to the side of my head, some kind of finger poke to some pressure point that made my left leg go all giggly. It was the sidekick to my face where I started tasting blood. It was the old-school bar room punch to the fucking mouth where I felt the blood start dripping from the corners of my mouth.

Those black belts were earned.

I don't remember how long it lasted, but it must have been a while. They dragged me to the stage and tossed me down where I managed to pick myself up onto all fours. I looked toward the door and Gretchen was gone. That was for the better. The four goons who escorted us in were there watching with satisfied smiles on their faces. Gretchen's AK was gone, but the one still had my M-60.

I felt my 1911s jerked from the holsters and tossed on the floor about ten feet in front of my face. I saw the stage lights glint off the nickel coat of Jammer's 1911.

I watched was Gretchen's mother leaned over the rail separating the stage from the choir loft and stand with a sword. It had a three-foot blade, at least two inches wide, a blunt tip, and no cross guard. It wasn't a sword for battle; it was an executioner's sword.

My plan had been to get Gretchen out of the line of fire, then get her mom as a hostage. Use it as leverage to keep these secret society assholes out of our lives forever. To be fair, I guess this was going the way all my plans go. What did they say about God laughing?

Her voice held the icy tone that could only be carried by a cryogenic containment unit filled with liquid nitrogen, or a disappointed mother. "Do you have any last words, Nick?"

Why would anyone ask that?

The hardwood floor was oddly rough under my palms. My knuckles were strangely sore, not that I'd have to worry about them cracking and scabbing over. I spat a hock of blood onto the hardwood before me, the red making a black smear against the cool teak. I felt the steel edge of the executioner's blade against the back of my neck, just above the collar of my dress shirt but below my hairline. Instead of thinking *I'm about to get my fucking head chopped off*, my thought was *that is uncomfortably fucking cold.*

"You really think I'm not going to fuckin' wreck your world?" I tried to growl, but it's hard to growl when you got a mouthful of blood.

I felt the angle of the blade on the back of my neck slightly shift. "Do you really think you're in a position to make threats?"

"Promises, bitch." I felt a string of blood drip from the corner of my mouth. "Fucking promises..."

"You brought this onto yourself." Again she hit me with the disapproving, disappointed mom tone. The joke was on her; with my life, I had grown immune to disappointed mom voice.

I couldn't help but chuckle. "Social Distortion song."

"Excuse me?" she asked almost pleasantly.

I tried to smile as the name of the song came to me. *"Story of My Life."*

Apparently, she wasn't going to monologue and she was tired of my, hopefully, pithy conversation. "Last words, Decker?"

Last words are a fucked up thing. Most people don't realize they're about to have their last words. I guess we always assume there is more time for that kind of thing. I knew I was on the spot.

"If You Know What I Mean, by Neil Diamond," I belatedly add: "Worthless, goddamned bitch."

She shook her head and her fingers milked the grip of the blunt tipped executioner's sword in her hands.

"Really? Neil Diamond?" She obviously ignored the profanity aimed at her. Fuck Shakespeare for setting the bar on last lines so fucking high. For every *The Rest is Silence* there are a thousand *What Bus's?* I guessed I could have, and should have, gone with, *The Rest is Silence.*

She shook her head and her fingers milked the grip of the blunt-tipped executioner's sword in her hands. "Really? Neil Diamond?" She obviously ignored the profanity aimed at her.

Fuck Shakespeare for setting the bar on last lines so fucking high. For every *The rest is silence,* there are a thousand *what buses?*

I guessed I could have, and should have, gone with *The rest is silence*. Goddammit.

They had no way of knowing that this was not even near the worse thing that had happened to me that day.

And then, over the expensive sound system of the megachurch, I heard the music.

Chapter Twenty-Six: If You Know What I Mean

If You Know What I Mean by Neil Diamond

It started with a soft piano melody. It drifted like a rowboat on a peaceful lake. It was a car ride on a well-paved road in a gorgeous mountain pass. It was soft and tender like the nonchalant caresses of old familiar lovers. It was Jammer's favorite song.

I looked up along the keen blade to the cold dark eyes of Gretchen's mother, which were as empty as a vacuum. For Gretchen to turn out the way she had her father must have been amazing because her mother was a bitch. I smiled as a look of confusion crossed her face the voice of Neil Diamond softly sang from the sound system.

When the night...

"Last chance." I smiled, and there was nothing charming about it as blood oozed from the corner of my mouth. The first two lines of the song were near poetry. I spit again and managed to get her slipper with a hock of blood.

The third line was patience, pure patience.

She raised the blade and without any pause or hesitation swung with all the might her well-chorded arms could give it. I thought about Switch lying in a hospital somewhere between life and death. My right hand shot up wreathed in fire as I grabbed the executioner's sword. The fire of my hand flared and I twisted my wrist, snapping the blade. No one was more surprised than me.

Neal Diamond had a great voice, but at that moment there were no *peaceful sounds* in or around me.

I pumped my legs and hurled myself forward and snatched both the 1911s, mine in my left and Jammer's in my right hand, as I rolled onto my back. I used the lip at the edge of the stage as a brace and the world snapped into the focus and everything went slow as I felt the power of the Sword flow into one perfect shot. The empty shell casing shot from my 1911 and arched a few feet in the air catching the stage lights. The round traveled in a light parabolic arch over a hundred yards in length. I never would have made the shot without the focus the Wrath provided. But the shot was made. The goon holding the M-60 caught the bullet right in the bridge of the nose and blew the back of his head all over the church pew behind him.

While Neal Diamond was smoking and polishing off a libation I was in the middle of some shit.

My right hand with Jammer's .45 shot up and out at an angle covering down on Gretchen's mother, who finally had a look on her face I could appreciate—it was the perfect welding of disbelief and horror.

I rolled to my left and off the stage. My feet planted on the floor and I got Jammer's gun back on target. Gretchen's mother had moved a few feet but stopped as the pistol came back into aim. I was only about twelve feet away and the two snapshots were easy even without the Wrath. I shot her through each thigh with Jammer's pistol. The rounds passed through the outside well away from the bone, but she fell bleeding just the same.

While Neil Diamond wanted to feel something again I felt the Wrath pulling at me. *It* wanted to kill them all. *It* wanted to burn the damn church down.

I felt the tingle in the back of my mind and ducked as I spun and started scurrying along the front row of pews. Wood chips flew up from the pew and stage lights exploded as submachine gun fire raked the front of the sanctuary. I popped up long enough to cook off one round from my .45 and missed as badly as a virgin at his first thrust for glory.

Neil Diamond wanted to know if she could make out the sounds, but I was too busy to notice.

I dove and rolled into the main aisle toward the door coming up in a crouch as the fire over me stopped. I looked back and saw one of the ninja girls land off the stage and try to cover the distance between us before I get around. It didn't matter. The round caught her in the shoulder and spun her like a top. I glanced up into the balcony and saw Gretchen with the AK-47 to her shoulder as she stood outside the sound booth. She started popping bursts at the stage, forcing the ninja girls to take cover in the choir loft.

Neil Diamond wanted to know if the aforementioned "she" could recollect their adventures in the TARDIS.

I stayed hunched over and moved as fast as I could under the edge of the pews. I popped up and focused the Wrath as I fired at fifty yards, shooting a goon through the ear as he tried to pick up the M-60. I ducked back low and kept moving as submachine gun fire blasted splinters from the pews.

The chorus was glorious, absolutely glorious playing over the speakers of the megachurch.

The large door opened and I saw a goon rushing in with a shotgun and a confused look on his face. The confusion was replaced with a moment of pain and then horror as I got a good aim with Jammer's pistol and shot him. I missed his mouth, which I was aiming for, but shot him through the throat which did the job just as well.

Neil Diamond sang about the cost of a dream while I kept moving. I knew if I stopped I was dead and Gretchen would be, too.

Switch might be dying. Jammer was dead. This was the only chance I'd have.

I knew I was getting close to the M-60 so I turned down a row of pews. The gunfire kept impacting, but now it was behind me. I heard a lull in the AK-47 fire and realized Gretchen must have been reloading up on the balcony. I popped up and saw I was five pews away from the two standing goons, and the double doors were starting to open. I didn't fire both pistols at once, even with the focus of the Wrath that was stupid. Jammer's pistol fired and caught the surprised man, firing forty-five degrees from where his target actually was, in his upper lip that bridge the bottom of the nose to the top of his mouth. I quickly aimed with my left hand and shot. The round caught the man in the upper chest but his plate carrier stopped it. I stepped up onto the pew and onto the pews back as I shot my right pistol again shooting him through his left eye.

Neil Diamond made a toast in his lyrics.

I saw men start to come through the double door and cooked off rounds as I ran over the pew backs to at least make them duck. Both pistols were empty as I dropped back to the floor between two pews. I could see feet under the pews. I took one of me MP-7s off the pew above me and loosed four bursts of three rounds and one of two before the magazine went empty. I shot three legs, who knows how many men they were attached to...

Jammer was dead. Someone had to pay. I knew it was my fault, all of it. But fuck me if they weren't going to feel it.

I heard the AK open up again.

I came up with the M-60 in my hands, stock to my shoulder. In the military doorways are referred to as "fatal funnels" and the four guys coming through the double doorway found out why. I cooked off a long burst, empty links and shells clattering against the pews and floor as the M-60 spat a cone of fire, the rounds forcing the four men to dance the horrible steps of the chain-gun-cha-cha.

That glorious chorus began again. It was Jammer's favorite song.

I spun and looked as the middle set of double doors opened. I got the M-60 on target and starting firing a three-round burst with each step as I moved toward it. The rounds punched through the *faux* wood doors and found targets on the other sides.

Neil Diamond asked if she remembered. I remembered, Neil.

I saw out of the corner of my eye as Gretchen jumped from the balcony and grabbed one of the purple plain cloth tapestry curtain things and started sliding down it. I assumed she'd emptied the second AK mag since she didn't have it with her. She hit the ground far more gracefully than I ever could and drew her pistols covering down on the double doors closest to her.

The sound system roared Neil Diamond and I would not be stopped.

I got to the aisle and turned my back on the doors and started sprinting toward the stage. I could still make this work. I watched as some of the ninja girls were making a move to get from the choir loft into the baptismal where I was guessing there was an exit. I starting cooking off bursts peppering the wall just under the crucifix forcing the ninja girls to duck back into the choir loft. Gretchen's mom was gone from the stage but from the smears, I could see she'd been dragged into the choir loft.

I didn't know what the song was about but it might have been about Neil Diamond losing his cherry.

I slowed my sprint to a walk as I turned to check my six, as I kept moving toward the stage. It was a good thing I did as I saw a goon sprinting toward me with a 12-gauge trying to get close enough to have it effective. The M-60 has a much farther effective range and three rounds into the man's hips crumpled him into a ball that slid and rolled across the carpet to a stop.

Neil Diamond paid the cost for a dream. I paid my best friend for what? A job? A greater good?

I came back around and put another burst into the baptismal as I saw one of the ninja girls look up above a choir pew to take a look.

I thought about Jammer and I wanted to unleash the Sword. I wanted to kill everyone in here and burn their goddamned gospel shop to the foundations then salt the sons of bitches. I wanted to subsume myself to the will of the Wrath and let it have its due in recompense for the cost of Jammer. It would have been so fucking easy. It would have felt so fucking worth it. I couldn't help but wonder if it wouldn't have been worth it?

Fuck all of it.

I ran and half-jumped, half-slid onto the stage. I spun and got my feet under me, coming up onto my feet without losing a lot of time.

I heard Gretchen call my name and I spun sinking down on my knee. She'd spotted a guy in the balcony with a rifle with a scope that was far too large to be practical in this auditorium. I put a three-round burst into him and he yelled before bouncing off the wall behind him then pitching forward to fall over the balcony rail.

Gretchen was sprinting toward me, one of her pistols holstered, the other in her hands reloading as she ran. Then I watched as she seamlessly switched. Anyone who doesn't think effective multitasking is sexy is insane.

Neil Diamond asked the titular question.

I moved to the choir loft and kicked the gate open. I saw two of the ninja girls who had kicked the shit out of me lying in the front row. I gestured with the barrel of the M-60. "Fucking move."

I herded them all into the back row. One of them had been trying to stop the bleeding of Gretchen's mother's leg wounds.

Neil Diamond repeated the question.

I looked at Gretchen's mom. "Call the fucking dogs off or you all die right here right now."

She angrily took a radio. "Stand down, I repeat, stand down."

Gretchen turned her back to her former sisters to watch the three entrances.

Neil Diamond repeated the question.

"Rip the sleeves off your karate outfits," I told them. "Wrap the wounds then wad up four of them and ram them against the entrance and exit wounds. Then take fresh sleeves, stretch them wide and wrap every fucking thing together tight."

Neil Diamond repeated the question.

Two of the girls got to work and I looked to Gretchen's mother, who was starting to look wan. "I had a buddy who could have patched you up lickity-split," I told her. "Now, you and I are gonna have a fucking conversation."

In the background, through the speakers Neil Diamond's voice and music drifted away as the song ended.

Yes, Neil, I know what you mean.

Chapter Twenty-Seven: Disappointed Mothers

Failure by Breaking Benjamin

She glared at me like I was the miscreant who was boning her daughter; so in that sense, it was probably fair. Even though the pain shooting from her shot legs she couldn't hide the disdain she felt for me. I didn't care for her either.

I kicked my left foot up on the pew and rested the M-60 on it as I reached under with my left hand to lift the Nut Sack. I could feel it was almost empty so I unclipped it and tossed it letting the twenty or so rounds that remained on the belt dangle. In an action movie, I could win a war with that belt—in reality, it'd be gone in two non-hyperbolic seconds.

"Is it me or Gretchen your teams have been coming after?" I asked as I took the gun back into a low-ready. I wanted it handy, but I wasn't trying to be threatening with it either.

"What do you mean?" Even though the disdain the confusion seemed genuine.

"The Tac Teams we've been running into," I told her.

"We've not sent teams after the two of you," she said with narrow eyes and contempt.

"Bullshit."

"When?" she asked.

"The assholes watching us while we were doing surveillance on Doc McDouche's apartment?"

"I didn't have teams watching you. I had a team checking out the Wedge Wood." Gretchen's angry mom sounded more confused than angry.

"When you fucking kidnapped Gretchen using the bikers as a distraction for the Tac Team." She glowered but said nothing so I continued. "Megatron's. There were the two plainclothes dipshits and then the two fire teams."

At first, it didn't dawn on Gretchen's mom what I was talking about then she finally asked, "Meyer? The hacker?"

"Yeah," I told her. "The Grand Vizier Megatron Terabyte the Cyber Samurai." In for a penny in for a pound, I guess.

"I sent an investigative team after we had hits of her tugging at threads on the Akashic Network," she confessed, biting her lip through the pain. "They went missing along with two teams that were sent for backup."

"What about the shitheads that fucked with us when we were grabbing Doc Douchebag?" I asked. I didn't know if she were lying, but she sounded convincing.

"We wanted him for his knowledge of the Spear. We located the Spear and retrieved it, and tried to secure Dr. Travis during simultaneous but separate operations." She glanced from me to the table where the Spear still sat.

"Gretchen," I said as calmly as I could with the rage pulling at me, but without taking my eyes off the nine ninja girls. "Grab that damned thing, will ya?"

Gretchen stepped over and knelt taking up the Spear in her hands. She gave it a twirl with the precision and skill of a good drum major in a college marching band. It seemed insanely well balanced and she gave it a few thrusts and swings that looked as intimidating as they looked combat effective.

"Gretchen, you can't let him have it!" her mother cried.

Gretchen stepped next to me and leveled the Spear at her mother. "Why?" There was genuine anguish in her voice. It wasn't that she had chosen a side; it was that she'd been forced to choose a side.

"If Hell has the Fiery Sword, Gretchen, we—humanity—we have to have a weapon of our own." Tears streamed down the woman's face. Part was the bullet wounds, but part of it was the betrayal of her daughter.

"Damnit, mother," Gretchen's voice sounded like she was pleading. "Hell doesn't have the Fiery Sword! Nick does."

"It's the same thing!" Her mother gasped.

I stared down one of the ninja girls who was starting to look squirrelly, gave my head a light shake, and nudged the barrel of the M-60 her direction. She tamed fairly quickly.

"It's not the same thing!" Gretchen cried. "If Hell had the Sword Armageddon would have come! If Heaven had the Sword Armageddon would have come! Nick having the Fiery Sword is the only thing, mother, the only thing keeping it from happening!"

I doubt she believed her daughter, I'm not sure that ice bitch believed anything other than position and power. But God love Gretchen for trying. I gave up on my family and my blood pressure dropped ten beats a minute. Gretchen hoped, she believed. Maybe that's why she was with me. She saw something more than the reality because I didn't see how the reality could be appealing.

"Who is the top dog?" I asked quietly.

"What?" her mother replied acidly.

"You're not in charge, so who is? Who is the top dog of your cute little Illuminati, Freemason, Tinfoil hat society?" I asked as I forced a smirk to lift the corners of my mouth. I wasn't feeling it, but I sure as shit would fake it.

"You won't get anything out of me," she spat.

I sighed. "Gretchen, who wears the big hat?"

"Elector Heinsius," Gretchen replied without hesitation.

I looked at her mother. "You have a line to Elector misspelled Ketchup?"

She bit her lip and glared.

I sighed. "Gretchen?"

"She would, yeah." Gretchen nodded and leaned against the shaft of the Spear.

"I raised you better than this!" she barked at her daughter.

"You raised a stripper, mother!" Gretchen spat right back.

I looked at Gretchen. "Hey…" Offended for her.

Gretchen looked at me and smiled. "Hashtag Feminism?"

"Yeah…" I sighed, "I got no real response to that." I looked to Gretchen's mother and covered her with the M-60. "Grab her phone and dial the guy for me, will you?"

I kept Gretchen's mother covered down with the belt fed as Gretchen got the phone from some pocked in the weird *gi*. Gretchen scrolled through the contacts and chose one, holding the phone out to me. I popped the bipod legs of the M-60 and sat it down as I took the phone and gestured for Gretchen to cover the others.

I hit dial and started walking off the stage, hopping off the edge as it rang. It rang twice as I started walking up the aisle.

"*Guten abend,*" the authoritative and masculine voice answered on the other side of the line.

"This is going to be a short fucking conversation if you don't speak English," I told him as I made my way to the aisle where the goons had been, and I walked down the row behind it.

"I do. To whom am I speaking?" He seemed neither pleased or displeased nor concerned that a stranger was on this line. The guy was the definition of dispassionate.

"Nick Decker." I took a gamble and added, "You've heard of me."

There was only the barest of pauses before he answered, "Indeed, Mr. Decker. To what do I owe the pleasure?" In that pause, I guessed he hit some kind of tracking or recording device or simple pulled up whatever files they had on me.

I held the phone between my cheek and shoulder as I bent over the back of the pew and picked up my spent 1911 and loaded a fresh magazine before dropping the slide. "You know where I operate, so let's just work with the assumption that when I say I have nine of your Sisters in Shadow including their local big wig under the barrel of an M-60 right now, you know who I'm talking about and that I'm not bullshitting."

"Indeed," was his only reply.

"Look, your organization has been butting heads with me, and when I say you have cost me dearly, that's not hyperbole. So we need to work out a system where we can keep out of each other's way."

"What do you suggest?" The voice almost seemed bemused, almost.

"Easy," I picked up Jammer's gun; I slid the magazine home and dropped the slide. I wanted vengeance; I wanted them to pay. I wanted every goddamned drop of blood they had. "You keep your people out of my city. You keep your people away from me. If me and mine ever see you and yours again, if I get a fucking whiff of you people, there will be hell to pay."

"And why should we abandon operations, Mr. Decker? Where is the *quid pro quo?*"

"Easy," I said as I slid Jammer's pistol into the holster in the small of my back. "I'm done dealing with your lot. I'm done killing your people when you get in my way. If I ever think you people are near me again, if I think your ass-bags are within a ten-goddamn-mile bubble of me... I'll give the Fiery Fuckin' Sword to Baal-goddamned-berieth."

There was silence on the other end of the line. It lasted long enough that I asked, "We get cut off?"

"No," was the terse reply I got.

"Cat got your fucking tongue?" I started walking back to the stage.

"You are bluffing, sir." His voice was steady, sure of its own certainty.

"Because of your people one of my oldest friends is laid up in a hospital right now and my best friend is dead." I didn't even hide the anger in my voice, the Wrath wanting to break free. "Try me, motherfucker."

There was another pause. Instead of climbing up onto the stage I took the stairs; it was a hell of a lot easier on the knees. "Agreed."

"How about you make it clear?" I looked at the hateful look on the face of Gretchen's mother.

Through the phone, I heard calmly and clearly. "You, Mr. Decker, and your associates will never be molested by, interfered with, or made any contact by any member of The Order of Brothers of the German House of Saint Mary in Jerusalem, or our Sisters In Shadow."

"For how long?" I growled.

"In perpetuity as long as you wield the Fiery Sword," he assured.

I bit my lip. "I'll keep this phone if we ever have to chat. But it's an 'I'll call you' not a 'You call me' deal. We clear?"

"Crystal, Mr. Decker." This guy's voice and demeanor were so level he could have been a tool for carpenters.

I hung up the phone and slid it in my pocket. I took out my flask and unscrewed the top and took two strong gulps. The Macallan 18 bit at the cuts in my mouth and I swallowed the Scotch with a good mix of blood. But it was worth it.

I met Gretchen's eyes and nodded. She smiled softly and took up the Spear and walked toward me. I picked up the M-60 and held it in my right hand and rested the feed tray up against my shoulder.

Gretchen interlaced her fingers in mine and we walked toward the stairs of the stage.

"Gretchen!" her mother called.

"It's finished, mom." Gretchen's eyes were locked to mine and she never looked back.

"DECKER!" her mother roared.

"If you don't realize I'm immune to disappointed mother bullshit you're out of your fucking mind, lady." The smirk on my lips was genuine. I stopped and leaned in, kissing Gretchen.

We'd freed ourselves of the Teutonic Knights, we'd found the Spear of Destiny, but the cost had been too high. I'd have rather lost with Jammer than won without him.

Gretchen ran upstairs to the sound booth and got my phone as I took a long drink of water from a fountain, spitting out blood, and taking another almost bloodless drink of Scotch.

We walked back across the parking lot, retrieving the Nut Sacks for the M-60, the AA-12 and the grenade launcher. Who knew that that stuff would come in handy? Hopefully, it never would, then again we could hope in one hand and shit in the other and I guarantee, which would fill first.

We got to the van and dropped the weaponry. We stood there and I pulled Gretchen into my arms. She wept into my suit jacket. I stroked her back and smoothed her thick hair, black as the ethereal void. With the depths I found in her eyes I knew there might never be a bottom to that well of tears.

We'd lost. No matter the tally, no matter the score, we'd lost. We'd lost things that could never be retrieved. It wasn't just Jammer that had left, but parts of us were taken with him. We would never again be as whole as we were.

I held her and she held me. She wept all the more because I couldn't. We'd both lost family today, her more so than me; or did she? So I held her, I just held her, because what else was there to do?

Epilogue: The Unexpected and Welcome Guest

Goodnight Saigon by Billy Joel

Skinny Craig the Bartender had cleared out the lunchtime crowd. There wasn't going to be a funeral here; Jammer's brother Christian was going to come to pick up Jammer's body and take it home. His sister who lived locally didn't show up to a strip club for a wake. Without the lunch crowd, it was just us, those who knew him. Paying our last respects to a man most of the world overlooked.

There was a bottle of Jameson sitting on the table and glasses. No flowers, no picture, nothing but the drink and our memories.

"He was a shitty tipper," Skinny Craig said as he lifted his glass of amber Irish liquid. "But he could have charged a lot more for the weed he sold. So I think I made out in the end."

"That's what she said." Ms. Hernandez softly wept even as she made the infantile joke that Jammer would have cackled over.

We all smiled and sipped the whiskey.

Joy with an E-Y wept, with Mary Jo and Gretchen on each side of her. The three of them held each other. Lucifer stood to my right and Yuri to my left. The large Russian wept unashamed.

Even though it didn't feel like it at the time Lucifer had been looking out for us. There was a reason cops didn't come looking for us after our massive gunfights and armed robberies: three words, Uncle Fuckin' Lew. But even that help hadn't saved my friend.

I saw a man standing in the corner. He had high patrician features and short close-cropped dark hair. His dark eyes were piercing. His suit was elegantly cut but held the air and shape of a military uniform. He held a package in his left hand, which could only be a bottle. He looked just like Jon Hamm, having stepped off the "Mad Men" set but without ten pounds of product in his hair.

Lucifer saw him and stiffened. Their eyes met. I put my hand on Lucifer's shoulder. "I got it."

I walked around the edge of the room coming toward the man. His eyes locked on me and followed me as I approached.

I felt the rage pulling at me. I felt the fire tickle over my hand. "Not here," I said quietly enough that only he and I heard it. "If we gotta let's take it outside."

He slowly shook his head. "Not today."

"Gabrielle's deal..."

"Not today." He said gently ending that line of conversation.

I nodded and stood next to him. "Why are you here then?"

"I was at the first wake for a paratrooper," he said with a soft solemnity, though his quiet volume couldn't hide the gravitas of his voice. "And I'll be at the last." I looked up and our eyes met. "I'll even be at yours, Nick."

"Thanks," I said quietly. I meant it.

"I don't like men who jump out of airplanes," the archangel said quietly. "But I love the ones who are willing to and fight."

"We love the things in others we see in ourselves, I guess," I said quietly as I watched Mr. Hernandez pantomime a story, the subject of which I had no earthly idea other than the hero was Jammer.

"Where is he?" I asked. "My Uncle wouldn't say."

Michael stood still as stone before looking to me with those eyes the color of what the sky should be. "In the Father's house, there are many rooms. Jammer is in one, I made sure of it."

I nodded gratefully. "Thank you."

Michael said nothing.

"There won't be for me, I don't reckon," I half-quietly chuckled.

"It's not looking like that's in the cards, Nick," he agreed.

We stood in silence. I felt Lucifer's eyes on us. "The Sword..." I started.

"Is the subject for another day," Michael interrupted adamantly. "Today is Jammer's."

"Do you drink?" I asked curiously.

He smiled for the first time. "I'm the Archangel of Paratroopers."

I reached over and nudged his elbow and motioned for him to come to the table. He did, reluctantly.

Skinny Craig filled the glasses and got a fresh one for the new arrival. I lifted my glass, and everyone clinked their glasses together as I toasted the only thing I could ever imagine the Commander and Champion of Heaven's Armies and the Master of all Hell's Legions agreeing upon.

"To Jammer."

About the Author

A veteran of the 82nd Airborne and a graduate of Auburn University. Dick Denny is a disappointment to his family, a fun guy to be around, and a handy guy to have about in a pinch.

Other Titles Available from Foundations Book Publishing Company

Hell for the Company

By Dick Denny

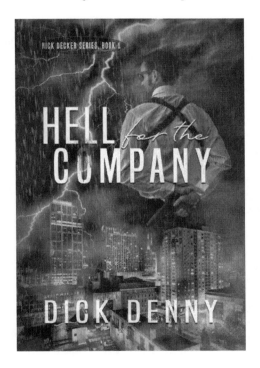

What stands between humanity and the battle of Armageddon? A word. But not just any sword - the Fiery Sword that guarded the Gates of Eden after humanity was kicked out.

Before the flood, it was stolen by the 23rd Demon kicked from heaven, who eventually married and imbued it into her human on. But now she'd dead, and it's starting to manifest.

Humanity's only hope? Nick Decker, a scotch-swilling PI armed with a .45 and the Wrath of God, his nerdy ninja-stripper girlfriend Gretchen, and his loyal acid-dropping, street-doc, war-buddy Jammer. It's up to them to keep the battle of Armageddon from happening...

—and find the Devil's lost dog.

Hellhound Bound

By D Thomas Jerlo

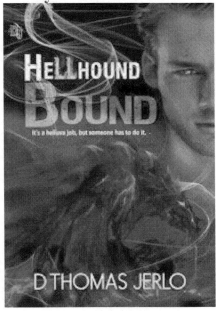

It's a helluva job, but someone has to do it, and for Rhune it's a small price to pay for his past sins.

He's taken a new name and a somewhat normal life, except at night when he transforms into a hellhound to take souls to the City of the Dead for purgatories legions to deliver them to Hell. For fifteen centuries he's lived in happy solitude until Hanna, a paralegal with the most amazing eyes, rear ends him in the small town of Rio Morden. He's seen those eyes before, but it's been years since the last time.

Now she's all grown up and involved in a murder trial that has its sights set on her becoming its next victim. What's a hellhound to do? Surely not fall in love—and certainly not with a Dreamwalker. And is that all she is?Mix in a diabolical lawyer and his lover, some Voodoo magic, and it's a recipe for mayhem and murder. Can Rhune keep Hanna safe, or is she destined to be Hellhound Bound?

EVIN

By A.S. Crowder

Eva has never seen the Forest of Evin, but her fate and the fate of the Forest may be intertwined.

Sinister forces seek to pull the Forest apart, and Eva may be the only one who can save it. Eva must travel between worlds to keep the Forest together...

...but the Forest of Evin thrums with power and the force tearing it apart may not be the only danger.

DECEPTION

By Laura Ranger

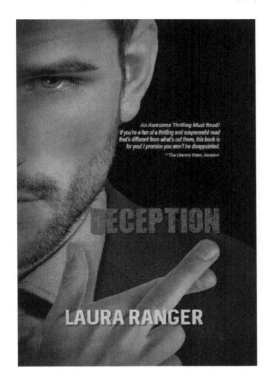

Izzy's had a lifetime of liars make up her past. All that changes with Caleb Matthews who's genuine and sincere. He teaches her not all is black or white. After 25 years of marriage she begins to suspect there's more to her husband then what she's known. No matter how she tries, she can't find anything amiss. I

s her paranoia from being deceived in her past sabotaging her future or is there something more she's missing?

Made in the USA
Lexington, KY
03 July 2019